Puffin Books

Graffiti on the fence

Hellz, Tan and Eddie are the local skateboarding trio. Every night after school they hang out together, terrorising the elderly Lallie, or 'the Witch' as they call her. They make their own rules, and give cheek to anyone who gets in their way.

But Lallie gives as good as she gets, and it is only when Hellz finds himself in her front garden one night, that he discovers she is the only one who can help him . . .

A new novel from the 1998 Winner of the Children's Book Council of Australia Award for Book of the Year (Younger Readers).

Also by Elaine Forrestal

The Watching Lake
Someone Like Me
Winning

Graffiti on the Fence

Elaine Forrestal

Puffin Books

Puffin Books

Published by the Penguin Group
Penguin Books Australia Ltd
250 Camberwell Road,
Camberwell, Victoria, 3124, Australia
Penguin Books Ltd
80 Strand, London WC2R 0RL, England
Penguin Putnam Inc.
375 Hudson Street, New York, New York 10014, USA
Penguin Books, a division of Pearson Canada
10 Alcorn Avenue, Toronto, Ontario, Canada M4V 3B2
Penguin Books (NZ) Ltd
Cnr Rosedale and Airborne Roads, Albany, Auckland, New Zealand
Penguin Books (South Africa) (Pty) Ltd
24 Sturdee Avenue, Rosebank, Johannesburg 2196, South Africa
Penguin Books India (P) Ltd
11, Community Centre, Panchsheel Park, New Delhi 110 017, India

First published by Penguin Books Australia, 1999

5 7 9 10 8 6

Designed by Cathy Larsen, Penguin Design Studio
Typeset in 11.5/17pt New Baskerville by Midland Typesetters,
Maryborough, Victoria
Printed and bound by McPherson's Printing Group, Maryborough, Victoria

National Library of Australia
Cataloguing-in-Publication data:

Forrestal, Elaine, 1941–.
Graffiti on the fence.

ISBN 0 14 130519 3.

I. Title.

A823.3

www.puffin.com.au

Acknowledgements

Horatius by Lord Macaulay, pages 14, 123, 124, 125, 126

A Jacobite's Exile, by Algernon Charles Swinburne, page 109

For Cameron and Amy
whose grandmother plays the witch

I would like to thank Peter Forrestal, but it was really his dog, Munch, who introduced me to the skateboarders.
E.F.

Alone stood brave Horatius
But constant still in mind;
Thrice thirty thousand foes before
And the broad flood behind.

from *Horatius* by Lord Macaulay

CHAPTER 1

'Go home, you adolescent rabble! It must be past your bed time!'

'Aw, shut up, you old bat!' Hellz shouts. He mounts his skateboard again, spinning and jumping it noisily up and down the kerbing twenty times or more.

'Yeah. We'll go home when we feel like it,' Tan yells, mirroring the moves that Hellz makes.

'And *you* can't stop us!' Eddie adds. 'We got rights. Same as anyone.'

'You've got no right keeping decent folks awake with your constant clackitty clack!'

'It's *your* stupid dog that keeps them awake!'

The old woman stands on her veranda. She raises her walking stick at them and shakes it angrily. But the rest of her words are drowned out by the frenzied barking of the dog as it leaps up and looks over the waist-high brick fence.

The three kids turn and skate back up the hill. Their bodies sway in unison and laughter bounces between them.

'Adolescent Scrabble,' Tan taunts, imitating the old woman's voice and actions.

'Prehistoric egghead!' Eddie shouts. 'Don't you know that *board* games are *boring*.'

'Except for skate*boards*.' Hellz grins, slowing to throw a play-punch at Tan's shoulder as he spins past. Tan groans dramatically.

'She's a witch y' know,' Eddie says when they are resting together on the crest.

'Yeaah. A *real* old hag,' Tan says, still smiling.

'No, seriously,' Eddie says. 'See all those zodiac signs and charms she wears around her neck? And she's always chanting stuff. Talkin' to herself. Y' hear her every day, out in her garden. And what does she *do* with all those herbs? Morton reckons she brews up magic potions. To put spells on people. She keeps pet spiders too – humungous ones.'

'Yeaah?' Tan says again, this time showing a real interest.

'He's full of bull – your brother.' Hellz is sceptical. 'How does he know anyway?'

''Cause he's been in her yard – gettin' his ball. He's seen her catchin' lizards. He reckons she chops them up and feeds them to the spiders – bit by bit.'

'Yuk!' Tan exclaims.

'She cooks them first,' Hellz says, stirring more than just his imaginary cauldron. He grins at Eddie who joins in with her own stirring motion.

'*That* must be what that awful smell is – coming from her house. Like burnt lizards and garlic!'

Tan's face goes pale.

'Hubble, bubble, toil and trouble,' Hellz chants, making his hands into claws that reach out for Tan. 'Turn them into *spider food*!' He lunges and the smaller boy ducks away.

When he stops laughing, Hellz picks up his board, does a double pirouette and sets off down the hill. 'Come on, guys,' he calls over his shoulder.

'Where?'

'To stir the witch's pot, a'course,' he says. The others mount their boards and swing in behind him in a perfect chain reaction.

A police car cruises around the corner. Hellz glides to a stop, but keeps one foot on his board, ready to ride. Eddie and Tan tip their boards up on end and slouch casually against the nearest fence.

The car pulls up beside them.

'I might have known,' one constable winds down the passenger window. 'It's the skate-boarders from hell again,' he says. 'I've warned you boys . . .'

'I am *not* a boy!' Edwina says furiously.

'He who flies with the crows must expect to be shot at,' the policeman mutters.

'*She*!' Eddie's voice rises by at least three deci-bels. Hellz shakes his head, trying to warn her.

'Are your parents at home?' the other constable calls from the driver's seat.

The kids nod.

'Then I suggest you head off there right now. If we get another complaint about the noise in this area you lot will be back at the station so fast you'll end up with jet lag.'

'But *we* ain't done nuthin,' Tan objects.

'This time, maybe,' the constable says. 'But if we do have to take you in, you'll be looking at more than just a caution – with records like yours.'

'It's *her* stupid dog makes all the noise.' Eddie, still seething, points towards the house on the corner.

Hellz says nothing. He gives the policemen a level stare. Then, tossing the lick of straight brown hair away from his face, he turns and scoots his board casually back up the hill. The others follow.

CHAPTER 2

'Where have you been?'

'Nowhere.'

'Angelo, I am *trying* to be patient. Now, don't lie to me.'

'We didn't *do* anything!'

'I'm not saying you did – *tonight.* But the police were here again. They want you off the streets by 8.30 p.m.'

'8.30 p.m! Do they want me to wear a nappy as well?'

Hellz's mother lifts her hands in a gesture of defeat and flops down into the lounge chair. In one corner of the room a TV couple gaze into each other's eyes as romantic music plays in the background.

Hellz goes into the kitchen and opens the

fridge. He drains the last of the Coke from the plastic bottle straight into his mouth and stuffs the empty container in the overflowing bin. Some left-over shepherd's pie sits gluggily on a plate. It's his least favourite meal, but he's starving. The last two slices of bread are for toast in the morning. He's already eaten the thin and curling crust.

Smothering the cold mince and mash in tomato sauce, he carries the plate to his room, sits on the edge of the bed and eats hungrily. The chair, pulled out from his desk, has all but disappeared under a pile of clothes. A computer screen rises from the debris on the desktop like the conning-tower of a submarine. Hellz adds his empty plate to an already precarious stack of comics and magazines. He puts on the headphones of his Walkman, lifts his only copy of *Rider* from where it has fallen on the floor and lies down on his bed. His walls are covered in posters and glossy magazine pictures of rock bands and leather-jacketed riders on shiny motorbikes.

'Hey, Hellz!' Tan runs across the school grounds to catch up with him. 'I checked out that old witch's place today.' Hellz stops. 'She's got a *big* spider all right!' Tan spreads his hands to dinner-plate size. 'I snuck up and touched the web with a stick and these *huge* hairy legs came out of the crack.'

Hellz gives a disinterested shrug.

'And guess what! She's got this enormous diamond hanging in her window!'

'Y' mean a crystal?' Hellz says.

'No!' Tan insists. 'The sun was shining on it and it flashed *all* the colours, just like a diamond.'

'Bet it's a crystal.'

'Bet it's a diamond.'

'Hi, guys,' Eddie joins them. 'Who's got a diamond?'

'That old witch on the corner of your street,' Tan says.

'Only it's a crystal,' Hellz says.

'They're magic, those crystals,' Eddie says. 'Y' c'n stare into them and *see* stuff – in the future, y' know?'

Several girls call to Eddie from the basketball court.

'See ya,' she says to Hellz and Tan, and runs to join Emma and the others. Even this early in the day she stands out from the other girls in their neat school uniforms. Her wild blonde hair refuses to be tamed by the mandatory headband and her sneakers make an individual statement that has already drawn fire from the deputy principal.

'Did the cops turn up at *her* house last night, too?' Tan asks.

'Dunno,' Hellz replies.

'My dad's goin' off his face. He's grounded me for a week and I didn't even *do* anythin' yet. But will he listen? No way! "We come this country and make new life," he says to me. "Work hard – no trouble with police." Great, innit? Makes y' wanna go out and trash somethin'.'

The siren mourns the end of recess. Tan slouches off in the direction of his classroom. Hellz drinks from the water fountain, taking his time. He savours the cold liquid in his mouth and throat, before strolling towards the room on the farthest corner of the cluster of buildings. It is tantalisingly close to a clump of low bushes and the main road. There is no fence.

He stands for a moment in the bright sunlight, smelling freedom. Then he turns and steps into the shadow of the veranda and through the classroom door. The teacher frowns at him but continues lecturing the class.

'You have, no doubt, heard media reports of an increase in vandalism and petty crime in this city. The notion of making parents more responsible for their children's behaviour has been around for some time, but now the community is demanding action. It seems that more and more young people are roaming our streets at night, when they should be at home studying ...'

Hellz gives an audible yawn from his desk at the back of the class. Everyone turns to look at him.

'... or, dare I suggest, Mr Hellios, catching up on their sleep.' Mr Sharp moves down the aisle and stops beside Hellz's desk.

'What?' Hellz glares up at him.

'You obviously have an opinion on this subject. Please, do give us all the benefit of your wisdom.'

The room is silent. All eyes are on him. Hellz swallows.

'Studying for what?' he says. 'There's no jobs anyway.'

There are some murmurs of approval and some sighs of *not again*. Mr Sharp returns to the front of the room.

'There will always be jobs for people who are prepared to work hard,' he says. 'But louts who hang about the streets at night, damaging other people's property ...'

'If they had somewhere to go, they wouldn't be out on the streets,' Hellz says.

'There are plenty of places for young people to go.' Mr Sharp waves his arm in the general direction of the city.

'If you've got money,' Hellz says.

'And why haven't they got money?' Mr Sharp asks the class. 'Because they're lazy layabouts, that's why. When I was young no one ever said to me, "Here's a hundred dollars, go out and amuse yourself." I've always had to *earn* my money ...' He's off again. It's his favourite subject. The Appalling Lack of Enterprise in the Young People of Today.

Hellz knows it's an argument he can't win. He tunes out the familiar voice and doodles with his pen. A cartoon picture of a tall, gaunt-looking witch emerges. She has wiry, shoulder-length hair that sticks out from under her hat. Her loose-fitting black dress floats out behind her as she flies through the air on a silver-handled walking stick. A boxer dog with a grotesquely squashed face rides pillion.

CHAPTER 3

Lallie is woken by a deep-throated growl. Winston is in the doorway with his hackles standing up like the bristles on a bottle brush. He gives a series of short, sharp barks. She sits up in bed, straining forward, listening.

The wind sighs in the tall trees that grow around her fence line. A branch of the thorny bougainvillea scrapes against her window. The house is big and old and creaky. It speaks to her with many voices. Until recently she knew them all. She listens again. Perhaps her hearing is not quite what it was. But she can rely on Winston. She knows he doesn't bark in the middle of the night without good reason.

She reaches for her walking stick with the heavy silver handle.

Winston prowls down the hallway. Returning minutes later, he crosses the room and slumps down beside the bed once more.

'Well done, Winston,' she says. The dog rests his rumpled face on the carpet. 'That scared them off.' His large brown eyes turn soulfully towards Lallie. '*Was none who would be foremost to lead such dire attack,*' she quotes. '*But those behind cried "Forward"! And those before cried "Back"!*'

She flourishes the walking stick, gripping it just below its curved, ice-pick handle and speaks to it in a serious voice. 'But, brave Horatius, there will be other battles. Winston and I may very well need your help, when the time comes.' She gives the stick an affectionate pat as she leans it against the head of the bed.

Her clock reads 4.30 a.m. She is wide awake. Picking up the book from beside her bed, she opens it at Lord Macaulay's epic poem and reads on:

In yon straight path a thousand
May well be stopped by three
Now who will stand on either hand
And keep the bridge with me?

When the birds in her garden begin to twitter and call, she gets up and pulls on her favourite loose black dress. Winston rises and shakes himself noisily.

'I suppose you want your breakfast,' she says, hobbling a little on stiff ankles. Winston races ahead of her and waits at the back door.

Lallie puts a handful of dry dog food into his bowl. While Winston eats enthusiastically, she goes out into her garden and gathers the fresh chamomile heads that she dries for making tea. As she stoops to pick the yellow heads, her eye is drawn to a bare patch of ground just inside her fence.

'Stay back, Winston!' The dog has already scoffed his meal. She catches hold of his collar and moves closer. 'Ah-hah. What have we here?' Winston tugs, but she holds him firm. 'A perfect print from a sizeable sneaker, wouldn't you say?' He looks at the ground. 'And since it's not one of mine, that only leaves you.' She pauses. 'But I haven't seen you wearing sneakers this week, Winston.' She coaxes the reluctant dog back inside the house and shuts the door. Picking up a steel measuring tape and a sheet of paper, she returns to the garden.

After measuring the print from toe to heel and across the widest part of the foot, she draws the tread pattern on the paper.

Back in the house, she says to Winston, 'Plaster of Paris would have been better. But this will have to do.' She places the paper carefully on the antique sideboard. 'Good of our visitor to leave a calling card, wasn't it? Now, what next? I suppose we should phone Herman.' The dog gazes up at her, tilting its crumpled-cushion face from side to side. 'No. You're absolutely right. He'll ooze in here like a jellyfish, lecture me about security, then go on and on about the delights of that old-people's home. And *I* won't be able to resist telling him to go and live there *himself*, if he thinks it's so desirable.' She bends one ear closer to the dog, who obliges with a whole string of conversational sounds from an expressive howl to a soft whimper. 'True, my dear. He's a good boy. But so boring. I mean you do expect accountants to mention money from time to time. But *he* seems incapable of talking about anything else. I often wonder how such a handsome boy could grow up to be so dull.' She strokes the top of Winston's head. 'Whereas you, my faithful Winston, have such a comical face. And you could not be dull if you tried.'

She switches on her electric kettle. The shelves in her open pantry are crowded with herbs drying in baskets, olives pickling in jars and a vinegar plant slowly digesting the remains of last night's bottle of red wine.

'Chamomile to stimulate the brain,' Lallie says, scooping some dried heads into a silver tea infuser. 'Now, here we have a puzzle, Winston. Someone comes calling. In the middle of the night. But nothing seems to be missing. Thanks to you scaring them off, no doubt. Notice the size of this footprint. Could it possibly belong to the tallest of our noisy skateboarders? The obvious leader of that loud-mouthed gang?' Her head nods on her wizened neck in answer to her own question. Winston, studying her closely, nods his head up and down in time with hers.

CHAPTER 4

'Hi guys. What y' doin'?' Eddie cruises her skateboard up to the two boys and spins a three-sixty-degree turn.

'Nuthin'.'

'Let's go, then.'

They get to their feet, lazily swinging their boards into position and adjusting their baseball caps. Hellz drains his Coke and sets the can down by the fence. Tan carries his with him. The two boys bend their bodies and push hard with their feet to catch up to Eddie. Six sets of wheels whirr and clack down the pavement as they race each other to the corner. Hellz jumps his board down to cross the road. The others follow.

On the other side of the T-junction the barrier kerbing offers a challenge. Eddie mistimes her jump and lands on her feet on the grass. Her board slews away, setting off on its own down the right-hand slope of the T. She runs to retrieve it.

'Good one, Eddie,' Tan laughs. 'Hey, it's great to be out again!' He punches the air with one fist and does a leaping turn.

'Yeah,' Eddie agrees. 'Feels like I was grounded forever. Wish *my* mum was as laid back as yours, Hellz.'

Hellz avoids her eyes. His mother has a new man. He can always tell. She'll be careful to keep him away from Hellz – for a while. Since their big fight over the last one Hellz *has* tried to understand. But she's vacuuming the carpets. And nagging him again, wanting him to tidy up his room. Not only that, she's *singing*. And she's even less interested in where he is, and what he is doing, than usual.

They push their boards up the hill, swing them around on the crest and begin the ride down again. Hellz suddenly leaves the footpath and zig-zags back and forth across the road. It's a blind hill. With the noise his board makes, he may not hear the sound of a car coming over the crest. But the added danger helps take his mind off other things.

As they approach the old woman's house, her dog rushes to the gate. Its barking becomes more and more frenzied as it leaps up and down inside the brick fence, following their progress for the full length of the block.

'Shut up!' Eddie yells as she sails past it. She crosses the T-road and jumps her board up, successfully this time, on the far side.

'Yeah, shut your ugly face!' Tan adds swallowing the last of his Coke and hurling the can at the dog. Winston yelps and Lallie's head appears, thrusting out over the gate.

'How dare you throw your rubbish in here!' she shouts. 'This is *not* the city dump, you know!'

'Coulda fooled me,' Hellz says, just loud enough.

'Yeah! Looks *exactly* like it!' Tan shouts, waving his hand towards the thick bushes that line her fence and hang like an awning out over the footpath.

'Don't you give *me* any of your cheek, young man!' Lallie's finger wags beside her now flushed face. 'The council built a skateboard track in the park – with *my* tax money. Go and use it!'

'Get lost, you old bag! We like this hill, don't

we, guys?' Eddie comes back across the road.

'Yeah,' Tan sneers.

Hellz stands defiantly silent, flicking his hair back and sticking out his chin.

For almost a minute they glare at each other across the gate. The old woman's grey hair bristles out from below the brim of her black felt hat. Her ankle-length dress hangs from her stooped and bony shoulders like a garment hung to dry on a wire coathanger.

Hellz turns his back, swinging his body and his board around in one sweeping, dismissive movement. With one foot gracefully stroking the pavement, he propels himself up the hill. Just ahead of Tan and Eddie.

Lallie is still standing there when they all come careering back down the path. Hair flying, shirts pressed against their bodies, faces grinning. Six empty cans from a kerb-side recycling crate are hurled in quick succession over Lallie's fence, narrowly missing her head.

'Right!' Lallie shouts. 'You'll regret this!' She hobbles up the steps and disappears between the creepers that grow up the sides and into the gutters of her wide veranda.

'Nair nair-ne nair nair!' Eddie shouts at her retreating back as all three riders take off down the sloping T-road. By the time the police arrive, there is no sign of them.

CHAPTER 5

'Can ya see the cops?' Tan asks.

'Yeah,' Hellz says, ducking his head back down behind the fence. 'In their car, down at the corner.'

'Losers!' Tan yells. Hellz grabs him and clamps his hand over the other boy's mouth.

'Shut up, will ya,' he hisses. 'I didn't bust a gut racing home the back way for you to invite them up here for tea and sandwiches!'

'Sorry.' Tan looks it. 'Didn' think.' He rummages in the sagging pocket of his pants and brings out a can of spray paint. 'Here, I brought ya this.'

'Where'd y' nick it from?' Hellz asks.

'Dad's shed,' Tan says. Hellz holds out his hand and Tan passes him the slim cylinder.

'Not much in it,' Hellz says, shaking the container against his ear.

'So?' Tan is irritated by this lack of enthusiasm. 'This is what we do, right? We wait until it gets dark, then we go down and tag her fence.'

'Not me,' Eddie says. 'I don't want to be grounded again. Not this week, anyway. It's the disco on Thursday night.'

'Oh, yeah. I forgot.' Tan looks deflated.

They hear the car engine start up, and quickly flatten themselves against the inside of the fence. They wait several minutes, then Hellz checks the road. Picking up his board and sliding the spray can into his own pocket, he does a few swoops and turns up and down the driveway, swinging his lanky limbs and directing the board with practised ease. Tan watches him, scowling slightly. There is room for only one skateboarder at a time in the narrow driveway.

Eddie pulls up clumps of grass with knobs of black soil clinging to their roots. She throws these at a mark on the brick fence, watching the particles scatter. Checking her aim.

'Angelo!'

'What?' Hellz looks up at his mother, standing

at the open door of the house.

'We're out of milk,' she calls. 'Run down to the deli and get some for me, will you?'

'And Coke?' he asks. She shakes her head and Hellz complains, 'Aaw! There's nothin' t' drink.'

'Oh . . . all right then,' Mum agrees reluctantly. 'But that will have to be the last until pay day.'

Hellz slips the coins that she hands him into his pocket where they clink against the spray can. He is a fraction taller than his mother, but they both have the same strong cheekbones and smooth olive skin. They could almost be brother and sister, until you look closely. Deeply etched lines around Mrs Hellios's eyes seem out of keeping with her otherwise youthful appearance.

'You comin'?' Hellz says to the others as he turns his board in the direction of the deli.

'Nah,' Eddie says. 'We're gunna have the best-sellin' band since the Beatles, right?' Hellz grins at her. 'I better go home and do me guitar practice.'

'Me too,' says Tan. He still feels cheated by Hellz's lack of praise for the prized can of spray paint. He wants to ask for it back, but Eddie interrupts.

'You don't even learn guitar,' she says.

'I mean homework,' Tan corrects himself.

'See y' then,' Hellz says over his shoulder as he mounts his skateboard and rides away down the hill. Tan gives the gate post a kick and watches him go.

Gliding along the edge of the road, just millimetres from the barrier kerbing, Hellz pictures Eddie playing guitar in their rock band. He sees himself standing at the microphone, drenched in sweat and admiration from the huge crowd. Tan is in the background on drums. Coloured stage lights transform Eddie's trademark checked shirt and bounce off her swinging blonde hair. Hellz has already asked his mother about learning guitar. But lessons cost ten dollars a week. Not to mention at least five hundred dollars for a decent guitar. Now she's spending her money on beer and dressing up for this creep, Rik! Hellz can see his dreams of a stage career evaporating. Along with owning a gleaming Harley Davidson, and joining the Hell's Angels bikie gang.

The street lights come on as Hellz reaches the deli. Once inside, he opens the refrigerated cabinet and takes out milk and a large bottle of Coke. The coins in his pocket only just cover the cost. Outside the shop he places his board on the pavement and pushes off, swinging the shopping in its plastic carry bag and wishing things could be the way they were before. When Rik is around, Mum seems happy. They laugh a lot. But Hellz can't forget the morning when Mum had an angry red gash on her face.

'What happened?' he had said, shocked at the damage to his mother's smooth skin.

'Nothing,' she'd said, without looking up.

'Mum!'

'It was an accident. Rik's ring collided with my cheek.'

'An *accident*?'

'All right, he'd had a few too many. We both had. Have you sorted out that mess in your room yet?'

Hellz wanted to warn her – tell her not to trust Rik. But he knew she would only get mad and yell at him. 'It's not easy for me, either, you know!'

He approaches the witch's corner and turns to go up the hill. The branches that hang out over the footpath join up with the street trees overhead to make a tunnel of darkness. At the far end, the street light throws weird, swaying shadows that move with the wind. Without the comfort of daylight and the noisy chatter of the others, Hellz feels his old fear of the dark returning. He consciously pushes it down, but it won't lie still and twists deep in his memory.

He could cross the street. Stay in the light. But there is no footpath on the other side. He would have to walk, or ride his board on the road again. In the dark, the risk of a car coming over the hill, too fast to avoid him, increases dramatically. But for Hellz the greater risk lies in giving in to his fear. He hunches his shoulders to control the shiver creeping up his back. Then he plunges into the moving shadows.

Hellz travels fast, keeping his eyes on the lighter patch of footpath at the end of the old woman's fence. He is almost through when an explosion of sound bursts beside his ear. The dog leaps at him out of the blackness. Its head appears, mouth wide, fangs and red eyes flashing, only centimetres away.

'Shit!' He drops the shopping bag. It hits his board. The board flips up and cracks him on the shin. As he hops and rubs his leg, the spray can jigs in his pocket. His hand closes over it. With great satisfaction he sprays *die dog* in huge, gold letters on the witch's brick fence.

CHAPTER 6

After school, as usual, the gang meets outside Hellz's house.

'Didn't ya tell ya dad it wasn't you?' Eddie asks the despondent Tan.

''Course I told him. He's not listenin', is he?'

Hellz gives the spray can back to Tan. 'It's still got some in it. Stick it back in his shed. Tell him it must have been there all the time.'

Tan looks hopeful for a moment, then his doubts swamp him. 'Wouldn't work.' He shakes his head. 'Dad knows *exactly* where everything is in that shed.'

'Worth a try,' Eddie says. 'You're already gunna miss the disco. What else can he do to ya'?'

'He'll think of somethin'.' Tan suddenly rounds on Hellz. 'Why did ya do it?'

Hellz shrugs. 'It was your idea.'

'Without *us*, I mean. It's *my* spray can. How come *I* cop all the grief and *you* have all the fun?'

'It just sorta happened, all right? The dog was goin' ballistic. The can was in my pocket. I just let fly.'

'Did the old witch see ya?' Eddie asks.

''Course not. By the time she got down her steps I was back home in front of the telly.'

*

'Just wait till I get hold of those kids, Winston! I'll teach them a thing or two.' Lallie scrubs at the paint scrawled on her fence. 'The police are worse than useless. No wonder people take the law into their own hands.' She gives up trying to erase the offending words. 'What we need is a battle plan – and a strong cup of tea.'

In her kitchen, Lallie opens several jars and mixes dried herbs in her tea pot. She pours in boiling water and stands, stirring and thinking as the distinctive aroma wafts towards her nose. After several minutes she strains the brown liquid into a cup and sits at the table, slowly sipping her tea.

The sun shines through the large, elongated crystal that hangs, suspended on a length of fishing line, inside her window. The shaft of rainbow colours, piercing deep into the heart of the room, twirls and hovers as the crystal swings slowly in the breeze. Lallie gazes at its mesmerising light.

'I know!' she says suddenly. Winston jerks up from his dozing position. He gives her a quizzical look. 'I've just had an idea.' She gets up and goes into the pantry. On the floor is a large cloth bag, half full of flour. She takes a ball of string from one of the shelves and ties the top of the bag tightly, using a bow and leaving one end of the string much longer than the other. Then she tips the bag upside down. 'Yes. That will do nicely,' she says when the string holds the flour in place. She carries the bag out to the front of the house.

Placing her stepladder close to the fence, Lallie climbs up and fastens the bag of flour, upside down, to a slender branch of the tree that hangs over the footpath. The branch swings down a bit with the weight of the flour, but the tied corners hold and a cluster of leaves still hides the bag. Lallie trails the long end of the string down inside her fence. Then she waits.

She hears kids coming home from school. The hum of voices. The occasional shout of farewell.

'Sorry, Winston,' she says quietly, as they approach. 'You'll have to stand guard *inside* for a while. I don't want you giving the game away.' She chuckles as she shuts him in the house. Checking that the trail of string is within easy reach, she takes up her position behind the fence.

At last she hears the clacking skateboards coming down the hill. She stretches up from her crouched position, and peers through a small gap between the trees and the overgrown bushes.

Hellz comes coasting down the path, picking up speed, just ahead of the other two. Lallie waits until the split second when the dark blur of his body closes the gap. Then she pulls the string.

'Yuk!'

'What *is* that?'

'Aaaaah!'

Lallie cackles delightedly behind the fence as three skateboards crash into each other and three squirming bodies lie tangled on the path.

'What *is* this stuff?' Tan stands up first, shaking a cascade of flour from his hair into Eddie's already powdered face.

'Aar-choo!' Eddie struggles to clear her breathing. 'What happened?' Hellz, still sitting on the pavement, points up into the tree where the empty bag hangs like an abandoned cocoon from the branch above them.

'Who put that there?' Tan asks.

'One guess.' Eddie points at the fence.

'Don't be stupid. *She* couldn't climb up a *tree*.'

'Maybe someone helped her,' Eddie says, calculating the distance from the branch to the ground with her eyes.

'Like the dog?' Hellz raises his eyebrows.

'Just look at this mess!' Tan is preoccupied with the state of his clothes, still streaked with white in spite of his vigorous brushing. 'I wish I'd kept that spray can,' he says. 'Y' wouldn't be able to *see* her fence for paint.'

Hellz tilts his head, listening. Waiting for the dog to bark. Everything is strangely quiet. He steps over to the fence and looks in between the bushes.

A wall of water hits him in the face as Lallie unkinks her hose. 'I'll give *you* paint! All of you!' she shouts and swings the hose to include Tan and Eddie. 'How dare you disfigure my fence with your disgusting graffiti! And what's more . . . ' she turns the hose back on Hellz as Eddie and Tan duck away, 'if I catch any one of you on my property, I'll sue your irresponsible parents for every cent they've got!' Lallie's voice follows the three kids as they take off up the street with wet flour turning to glue in their hair.

CHAPTER 7

'I *know* that this is the third time I have rung you this week, young man! If you were doing your job properly, *once* would be enough!'

'We *have* spoken to the suspects *and* their parents, madam. There really is nothing more we can do – unless we have evidence that a crime has been committed.'

'I told you. I *have* evidence.'

'A rough drawing of a shoe print does not, in itself, constitute evidence. Is the footprint still visible in your garden?'

'Of course it's not! But if you had bothered to come a week ago it would have been. Since then, my property has been invaded, my roof battered by stones and my fly-screens ripped apart! Not to mention my peace of mind.'

'But nothing has been stolen?'

'Three large stakes were stolen from the new trees the council planted along our street.'

'Then the trees are not on your property?'

'No. But, armed with lengths of four-by-two like that, these larrikins could *kill* somebody!'

'I'm sorry, madam. There is nothing we can do at this time.'

Lallie puts the phone down with a grunt of disgust.

'Well, Winston,' she says. 'The police are obviously not interested. I had hoped my own little plan would teach those kids a lesson. Instead, I seem to have spurred them on to even more dastardly deeds. I must be losing my touch.'

Winston goes to the door, whining, but wagging his stumpy tail.

'Who is it?' Lallie calls, rising to her feet. Before she reaches the door her son, Herman, comes in.

'Mother, I want you to meet Elliott Adams.' He ushers in a slightly built man in a grey suit.

Lallie holds out her bony hand. Elliott Adams takes it in both of his, bows his well-greased head of slicked-back hair low over it and says, 'Enchanted to meet you, Mrs Hagbert. Herman has told me *all* about you. And since we are bound to become *such* good friends, may I call you Lallie?'

The old woman peers at him. 'You may call me whatever you choose,' she says guardedly. 'And I shall reserve the right to do the same to you.'

'By all means, dear lady,' he says, glancing uncertainly at Herman. Then, with a thin, rather forced laugh, he bows again.

'Elliott is in real estate, Mother,' Herman says. 'And since you must agree, now, that you can no longer stay here, Elliott has come to help us out.'

'But I'm not going out, dear. I wouldn't dream of going out when I have guests! Do sit down and have a cup of tea.'

'I mean,' Herman says, leaning closer to his mother and pronouncing every word with great care, 'he'll get us a good price – for the house.'

'Oh, a *very* good price, my dear Lallie. Elliott's eyes light up. 'We have just the right . . . er, *buyer* – for this magnificent property.' He is smiling so broadly that Lallie thinks his chin is in danger of separating from the rest of his face. As he bows yet again, she looks at the floor, half expecting to see the man's lower jaw and teeth lying there.

Distracting as this image may be, Lallie does not allow it to put her off. 'I wish to remind you, young man,' she says firmly, 'that what you describe as "this magnificent property" happens to be *my home*!'

'Of course, my dear Mrs Hagbert. And a wonderful home it has been, I'm sure.'

'What do you mean, *has been*?' Lallie stretches her neck to its full length. 'And I am not your *dear* anything!'

'No! ... er ... yes ... of course.' The estate agent flounders.

'Living alone on this huge block of land just isn't safe any more, Mother.' Herman comes to his rescue.

'Nonsense!' Lallie objects. 'Stones on the roof, a damaged fly-screen and a bit of graffiti do not require an unconditional surrender. I wouldn't have bothered to call you, except that I thought you would have the phone number of the man who makes those security screens. Since we have to replace the damaged ones, we might as well do it properly.'

'Security screens do add value to a house,' Elliott Adams recovers enough to mend his fractured smile. 'They're practically standard, these days. But *you* don't need to worry about it. That sort of thing can be done *after* you move out.'

'Move out? Have I not made myself perfectly clear? I am *not* moving anywhere! It's just a bunch of kids who need to be taught a lesson, that's all. Now, *do* you have that name and number?'

Elliott shifts his feet and narrows his eyes. Herman shakes his head.

'Then I'll just have to look up the Yellow Pages,' Lallie says firmly. 'Now, what we *all* need is a cup of tea.'

'I need something stronger than tea,' Elliott Adams mutters.

Herman turns to Lallie. 'I *do* have the number for the security screens – at home,' he sighs. 'I don't suppose you have any *real* tea.'

'You mean those commercial floor sweepings that they put in packets and charge a fortune for? Very bad for your digestion.' Lallie goes into the kitchen and fills her kettle. 'Come to think of it,' she calls back over her shoulder, 'that's probably more than half your trouble. Poor digestion!'

Herman and Elliott exchange glances. As Lallie comes back, Herman looks at his watch. 'Oh. Is that the time?' he says. 'Sorry, Mother, we can't stay. I've just remembered I have an appointment.'

'Never mind, dear,' Lallie says. She follows the two men to the front door with her arms extended as if she were shooing chooks out of her garden. 'Don't forget that phone number,' she calls as they hurry out to the street. Herman waves and the two men get into the white station wagon that is parked beside the house.

'Thank goodness they've gone, Winston,' Lallie says. 'If they *had* stayed, I don't think I could have resisted putting something very unpleasant in that real estate agent's tea.'

CHAPTER 8

'There must be a law or somethin'. She can't just go round dumpin' flour on people – ruinin' their clothes and . . .'

'Shut up, Tan. I'm thinkin',' Hellz says.

Tan sits down despondently on the side of the road.

Minutes later Eddie says, 'I read a book about witches.' Two heads turn in her direction. 'Y' know, in the olden days, to find out if a woman really was a witch, they used to throw her into a lake. If she drowned, that proved she wasn't one. But if she survived, that proved she *was* one. So they went ahead and burned her at the stake.'

'Jeez, we don't wanna *kill* the old bat, just get her off our case, eh! We could set fire to her letterbox!' Tan says.

'Oh, sure,' Hellz says scathingly. 'With that African jungle she's got hangin' over her fence, the whole street would go up in flames.'

'Wow,' Tan says, picturing the blaze.

'Hey, *my* house is in this street!' Eddie objects.

'And mine,' Hellz says.

Tan looks embarrassed.

Eddie has a way of rolling and crossing her eyes when she's really thinking. 'What you have to do with witches,' she says, eventually, 'is take away their power.'

'How?' Tan asks.

Thought wrinkles clear from Hellz's face making way for his trademark grin. Suddenly he steps on his board and pushes it up over the brow of the hill, away from the witch's house. Within seconds Tan and Eddie are doing the same. It's not such a good run. Shorter. And there's a roundabout to negotiate. They jump their boards over two sets of kerbing, swinging their arms and swaying their bodies. Opposite the park they turn simultaneously and scoot several times, pushing with one foot on the ground. No words are needed. Like a school of fish they travel together, very fast, in one direction. Then, for no apparent reason, they turn as one and travel just as fast the other way.

They arrive back at their starting point – the paved driveway outside Hellz's house. He flicks his board up, catches it in one hand, and sits on the low, brick fence. Eddie flicks her board up in the same way. Tan does a quick cut and turn before joining them. Hellz notes the challenge in this breakaway action, but he doesn't take it up.

He sits, staring straight ahead, chin raised and eyelids half closed. Eddie toys with a pebble. Tan loses patience first.

'We just gunna sit here?' he asks. Hellz continues his fixed stare for several more minutes. Then he pushes up the peak of his baseball cap.

'Nope,' he says. 'We're gunna steal her crystal.'

Eddie gasps. 'Steal her crystal? You mean the one *inside* her window?'

'When y' gunna do it?' Tan asks.

'Y' mean, when are *we* gunna do it?' Hellz applies the pressure. 'I'll need a bunk up.'

'But that window is right on the street!' Tan says. 'Anyone going past could see us.'

'Not if it's dark,' Hellz says.

'It's never dark there. The street light is right outside that window.'

'And what about the dog?' Eddie adds.

'Chicken are ya?'

''Course not. I just don't wanna get done for stealin'.'

'I'm not plannin' on gettin' done. Just gettin' her back!' Hellz says.

'It's a bit . . . y' know . . . dangerous,' Eddie says. 'Stealin' a crystal off a witch.'

'You got a better idea?' Hellz drop-kicks a sod of earth over the fence. They all watch it breaking up in mid flight, dropping miniature bombs that explode on impact and leave the path splattered with brown marks. 'So, who's in and who's out of this one?'

Eddie and Tan look at each other.

'I'm in,' Eddie says.

'I'm in,' Tan says, wondering how he will manage to sneak out of the house after dark with a father who watches every move he makes.

'Right. This is what we do . . . ' Hellz says, before Tan can change his mind.

After dinner, Tan arrives at Hellz's house. Hellz meets him at the door.

'Y' took y' time,' Hellz says, but quietly.

'Dad was a bit suspicious. But I told him I need to go over some homework with you. Is Eddie here?' Following Hellz's lead, Tan speaks in a whisper.

'I said I'd phone her when we're ready. She'll tell her folks the homework story and meet us at her gate.'

Tan follows Hellz to the phone in the hallway. Eddie answers. So far, so good.

Hellz's mum is engrossed in her favourite TV show. Tan and Hellz close the door quietly as they leave.

They find Eddie waiting in the shadow of her imposing gatepost, and all three stroll on casually across the road.

Outside Lallie's house, Hellz produces a stone from his pocket, takes aim at the street light, and throws. The stone bounces off the metal shade. It makes a small tinging noise and comes to rest on the grass. Hellz picks it up and tries again. This time the globe breaks with a crash. The sound of shattering glass is so loud that he looks around, expecting the whole street to come out and investigate.

No one comes. They stand together in the darkness. The whites of Tan's eyes are all Hellz can see of him. Eddie's lighter skin and blonde hair make her more visible. He should have told her to wear a parka with a hood. But it's too late to send her back now.

'Okay, Eddie, remember what I told you. Stand where you've got the best view and whistle if anyone comes.'

Eddie nods.

Hellz takes the long screwdriver from his pocket. He positions Tan under the window with his back bent and his hands braced on his knees. Hellz climbs onto Tan's back and reaches up, catching hold of the window ledge. Tan wobbles, but manages to keep his balance while Hellz stands on his shoulders.

He feels for each screw and, twisting quickly, removes the security screen and slides it to the ground. There is music playing inside the house. As usual, Lallie has the volume turned up. Hellz feels Tan becoming more unstable beneath him and jumps down, just as Tan's legs buckle. On all fours, Tan hisses, 'Jeez, you're heavy.'

'I'm not done yet.'

'I am,' Tan says emphatically. 'Make dents in Eddie's shoulders for a while.'

Eddie glances quickly up and down the hill, then moves closer to the two boys.

'What's up?' she whispers.

'Muscleman here says I'm too heavy. D'y reckon you can hold me?'

'Sure,' Eddie says.

'Okay, swap with Tan.'

Eddie's strong body supports Hellz, but she is a bit shorter than Tan. Hellz slides the screwdriver blade under the window frame and levers it upwards. Behind its security screen the window is not locked. Hellz eases it up and reaches in for the crystal. It is half a centimetre away from his outstretched hand. He'll have to get down and climb on Tan's shoulders again.

At that moment the sound of barking erupts inside the house as the dog rushes to the window. Hellz launches himself desperately at the crystal, yanks it down and falls to the ground – on top of Eddie.

The face of the old woman appears in the window as they struggle to their feet and run like mad.

CHAPTER 9

Lallie storms up the hill. Her stiff old legs propel her gaunt body with determined speed. Her walking stick delivers a series of angry blows to the pavement. Winston trots protectively at her side, head up, ears swivelling.

Lallie thumps on the door of the house where she most often sees the three kids. There is no response. She thumps again.

'Who is it?' a woman's voice calls warily from inside.

'Lallie Hagbert.'

Above the music of the television, another voice says something to the woman in the house. She shouts, 'Leave us alone! It wasn't him.'

'I saw him! And his two mates. They need a good hiding – all three of them.'

The door slowly opens, stopping halfway. Hellz's mother stands with her arms across her chest, filling the opening.

'Are you threatening my son?' she demands. Hellz's face appears over his mother's shoulder.

'I'll do more than threaten him if he comes anywhere *near* my house again.'

'Push off!' Hellz says vehemently.

'Not without my crystal.' Lallie glares first at Hellz then his mother.

'What crystal?' Mum says.

'The one your son stole from my house just now.'

'He was here all evening. Doing his homework.'

'I very much doubt it,' Lallie says. 'Hand it over.' She looks directly at Hellz and holds out her hand.

'He said he hasn't got it! Are you deaf or something?' Mum plants her hands on her hips.

Still looking directly at Hellz, Lallie says quietly, 'You will regret this, young man. That is no ordinary crystal. It has been known to save lives. But it is also capable of snuffing them out. Just like that . . . ' she reaches out and snaps her long fingers right under his nose, '. . . with its special powers.'

'What powers?' Mum says. 'You can buy crystals like that at the markets for twenty dollars.'

'Oh, so you *have* seen it!' Lallie says triumphantly.

'Everyone in the street has seen it hanging in your window.'

'Well, it's not there now,' Lallie declares. 'And until it is returned, someone will be very uncomfortable, to say the least. Appearances can be deceptive, you know. It's probably burning a hole in *his* pocket right now!' She stabs an accusing finger at Hellz. Mum leans sideways to avoid the long arm in the swinging sleeve.

Hellz feels uncomfortable under the heat of Lallie's stare. But he can't look away. His mother tries to push the door closed, but Lallie places her extended hand flat against it. There is more force in Lallie's ancient body than Mrs Hellios expects. For a long moment they confront each other.

Then Lallie turns away. 'Don't think I've finished with you yet,' she says menacingly, and stalks off down the path.

Out of sight of the Hellios house, she rests heavily on her stick. 'I suppose one can't blame a mother for trying to protect her son, Winston,' she says. 'But I fear for this younger generation. Where will they learn to respect other people's rights?' Winston regards her curiously. 'Certainly not from mothers like that!'

CHAPTER 10

'What was all that about?' In the doorway, Mum turns to Hellz.

'Dunno,' Hellz shrugs.

'Silly old bat. She's probably put her precious crystal down somewhere and forgotten where.'

'Probably,' Hellz agrees. The crystal sits heavily in his pocket.

Hellz wakes, terrified and drenched with sweat. He lies rigid in his bed, listening intently. Gradually he moves his eyes around the room. Everything appears familiar and normal in the early morning light. But his body refuses to relax.

He finds Mum in the kitchen with the newspaper spread out in front of her.

'You look terrible,' she says, looking up.

'Thanks, Mum,' Hellz nods.

'Are you okay?'

'Had a weird dream, that's all.'

'What about?'

'He came after me. I ran and ran but . . .'

'What?'

'He killed me.'

'Who?'

'I don't know. It looked like . . . I don't know. He had a knife and . . .'

'And . . .?' Mum's voice urges.

'It was *really* weird. I could see myself, lying there, dead. I was standing in the shadows, looking down at my own dead body.'

'That really *is* weird.'

'There's more. You know that . . . that sort of skeleton – with the scythe thing?' Mum wrinkles the skin on her forehead. 'The one that wears the long black robe, with the hood . . .'

'What? The Grim Reaper?' she laughs dismissively and returns to her newspaper. When she looks up, Hellz is still standing there. 'Don't worry about it.' She pats his arm. 'Only a dream.'

Hellz goes back to his room and picks up his

school bag. He takes the crystal from under his pillow and puts it into his top pocket. It makes a hard ridge against his heart. He doesn't want to be caught with it on him, but he can't leave the evidence lying around, either. Mum is about to go into one of her cleaning frenzies. He can tell.

Tan reckons the crystal is worth a lot of money. But even if Mum is right and he only gets twenty dollars for it, that's better than nothing. He takes it out and looks at it again. Although the outer hexagonal shape is clear and transparent, there is a twist of something opaque at the centre. As if, long ago, a small flaw in the glass has let in some substance that has become trapped inside. This central core seems to be constantly moving. Restless to get out. When he peers into it, he finds it hard to look away.

They have assembly first up. The principal comes to the microphone.

'The owner of a burgled house in Hastings Street has contacted me. She believes she recognised students from this school leaving the scene of the crime. This is a very serious matter. The police would like to talk to anyone with information.'

Hellz keeps his head down as they file back into class. He knows he will have to get rid of the crystal quickly. He'll wag school after lunch and take a bus into town – where the markets are. His chest begins to feel hot. The skin is tight, as if he is sunburnt. He moves the crystal from his shirt to his jeans pocket. The burning feeling subsides. Hellz leans back in his chair with a smile of relief.

'What are you laughing at, Hellios?' Mr Sharp asks.

'I'm not laughing.'

'Good. Because I don't find the Roman Empire the least bit funny. Now get on with your work.'

Hellz tries to concentrate on the intrigues of Julius Caesar, but the crystal is heating up again. Warming through to his leg. What was it the old witch said? He tries to remember. But there's a burning sensation travelling up his left hip, cutting into his flesh like a knife. He shifts in his seat. The pain shifts a little, but it pushes everything else out of his mind.

At recess time Tan sits beside Hellz in the teeming playground. He takes a spring roll out of his lunchbox. The distinctive smell of soya sauce wafts up towards them, making Hellz's mouth water.

'Did you get rumbled?' Hellz asks.

'No. I was lucky for once. How about you?'

'The old witch came bangin' on our door,' Hellz says. Tan sucks in a quick, anxious breath. 'Reckons she saw us.'

'Far out! So it *was* her they were talkin' about at assembly. *Now* what're we gunna do?'

'It's okay. Mum told her to get lost. Said I was home all evenin', doin' homework.' Hellz gives a short, but somehow unconvincing laugh which is echoed, nervously, by Tan.

'Where's the . . . you know?'

Hellz pats his pocket.

'What do y' reckon we'll get for it?'

'Dunno.'

'It's a real diamond, y' know. They're worth heaps!'

'Mum says y' can buy them for twenty bucks at the markets.'

'No, they're just fake ones at the markets.'

'How d' y' know the difference?'

'Easy,' Tan skites. For once he knows more than Hellz. 'Real diamonds can cut glass,' he says. 'Let's test it on the window over there.'

'Oh, sure,' Hellz says scathingly. 'Why don't we just put up a sign? *Testing stolen crystal. Police informers welcome.*'

'I didn't mean *right now.*' Tan tries to save face. 'Later. When no one's around.'

The Roman Empire is followed by algebra. No matter where Hellz puts the crystal, it burns him. He tries to concentrate on the money and what he will do with it. He'll have to share it with the others. But he's taken most of the risks – done most of the work. Under cover of his desk he swaps it from one pocket to the other. Within minutes it's pricking and burning again, driving him mad!

He begins to wish that he had left it hanging in the witch's window after all. No matter how much money it's worth, he just wants to get rid of it. But where? The big dump-bin near the gardener's shed? Maybe, if he wraps it up, no one will notice it amongst all that rubbish. He'll just have to make sure no one sees him.

He leaves the classroom as if he's going to the toilet, but heads for the dump-bin instead. Just as he reaches it, the music teacher comes past.

'What are you doing out here in the car park, Angelo? Shouldn't you be in class?'

'Yes, Mrs Young.' He can't risk it now. Abandoning that plan he heads back towards his classroom.

The crystal seems to have doubled in size. It feels heavy and obvious, weighing down his pocket. Mr Sharp is bound to notice the bulge dragging his jeans down on one side. He is not supposed to wear jeans to school. But Mum hasn't done the washing for over a week. She's too busy cleaning the house. The principal is sending her a note about uniform policy – again.

'Ah, you've decided to rejoin us at last, Angelo,' his teacher says. 'We won't ask where you've been in case you tell us. But I expect that exercise to be *finished* today, you understand.'

The crystal throbs against his leg.

CHAPTER 11

Sitting in the classroom with the teacher's voice washing over him, and the small sighs and fidgeting movements from the other desks masking his restlessness, Hellz fights to ignore the crystal in his pocket. It seems to be giving off more and more heat. What if it gets so hot that it burns right through to his skin? He can't resist checking for holes in his jeans. There are none – yet. But he expects to see smoke at any moment.

He takes it out and holds the crystal in his hand. His leg cools but his hand burns. He drops the facetted glass back into his pocket. Two red lines mark his palm with the distinctive oblong shape. He feels ill.

'I shouldn't bother reading your palm, Hellios. I can tell you *exactly* what your future will hold if you don't pay more attention in class.'

'I don't feel well.'

'Is that so? And what seems to be causing this sudden illness? Do I detect an allergy to algebra?'

'I . . . don't know. I feel . . . hot.'

Mr Sharp stands beside Hellz and peers at him. 'Hmm. Go and drink some cold water.' Hellz rises shakily to his feet and crosses the room. 'And wash your face,' the teacher calls after him.

Hellz goes to the drinking fountain and gulps down the cold water. Then he pushes open the door to the toilet block. The searing heat is travelling up his leg and spreading into his intestines, his bowels, his spine.

He lurches into the nearest cubicle, pulls the crystal from his pocket and drops it into the toilet bowl. He leans on the metal button, holding it flat against the concrete wall. Water leaps and splashes and swirls into the stained bowl. The crystal disappears under the frothing torrent.

Hellz closes his eyes. He feels the hot blood draining away from his head as he rests against the wall's cool roughness. At last he is free of the thing. He wonders, briefly, how much money he would have got for it. But tells himself that it would have to be a lot – like a million dollars – for him to go through that again.

Feeling calm now, he opens his eyes. The crystal sparkles up at him from under the still water.

Hellz swallows hard and flushes the toilet again. But the cistern has not had a chance to fill and the thin stream of water barely coats the sides of the bowl, eddying harmlessly around the accusing glass eye.

He turns away. Let someone else find it. There are two hundred kids in the school. Anyone could have dropped it in there. But as he comes out through the cubicle door, Stephen Oliver confronts him.

'Mr Sharp sent me to see if you are okay,' the smaller boy says.

'What?' Hellz stands frozen in the doorway.

'Are you okay?' Stephen says again.

'Oh. Yeah. Must be somethin' I ate.' Hellz retreats into the cubicle and locks the door behind him. He dives his hand into the toilet bowl, pulls out the icy crystal and flushes the toilet. Pulling off a long strip of toilet paper, he wraps it round and round the glinting glass and shoves it into his pocket. His jeans tighten around the bulge.

Stephen stares curiously at him as he emerges from the cubicle.

'Get outta here,' Hellz says gruffly. 'I c'n wipe me own bum!' He washes his hands in the basin, flicking some of the water at Stephen as he goes out the door.

The final siren sounds at last. Hellz slips away across the oval. He walks quickly, shielded from the school by the dense line of shrubs until he turns the corner. All he can think of is getting away by himself. To work this thing out. Even through the layers of toilet paper, the crystal feels alive, pulsing and burning in his pocket. He has to get rid of it. But how?

His mind has gone blank. A tiny voice from somewhere in his subconscious says *bury it.* But where? His immediate landscape is full of walled gardens and concrete footpaths.

Reaching his own gate, he remembers a bare, sandy patch of ground up behind the garden shed. But he'll have to be quick – before Mum gets home. He begins to run. His chest heaves as he gasps for air. His jeans pull tighter against his leg. The throbbing crystal demands more attention with every stride.

CHAPTER 12

At the top of the driveway, Hellz throws his school bag over the padlocked side gate and climbs after it. When he drops to the ground, he is a few steps from his mother's bedroom. The window is above his head, but he can hear movement. Lifting his bag slowly, he listens.

He pictures a burglar, raiding his mother's dressing table – pulling out drawers. He hears the scraping sounds of wood against wood. In, out. In, out. Then a low groan.

His first instinct is to run away. Then to get help. Run to the phone box. Call 000. Not the police, though. They'd never believe him. They'd search him and find . . . No!

The fire brigade! But what would he tell them? He stands on tiptoe. But he still can't see into the window. He imagines the burglar: big and heavy, wearing a balaclava. Suddenly he's angry that anyone would dare to touch his mother's things. He runs up the path to the back door, fuelling his outrage by picturing her brightly coloured underclothes scattered and her cheap, but colourful jewellery trampled and discarded.

There is no money in the house. There is never any money, these days. But when thieves don't find money, they trash the place. He should know. After Mum's room, his is sure to be next. He can already see his posters being ripped from the walls and his skateboard smashed in two.

He reaches the back door. It stands wide open. The burglar must have forced it. Nothing in the kitchen has been disturbed. This is definitely a pro. Only after money. He stops. Will he have a gun? Will he shoot first and ask questions afterwards?

Hellz hears voices. There are two of them. The images in his mind blacken as a new thought occurs to him. He creeps across the room, every muscle tight, all his senses on alert. It's his mother's voice.

The tension suddenly goes out of his body.

He gives a short snort of disgust. The other voice belongs to Rik.

Why are they here at this time of day? Mum didn't tell him she'd be coming straight home. She must have told Rik, though. He feels angry again. He thinks about the present Rik bought him the other day. That huge book about stars and planets.

'What's he trying to do? Educate me?'

'Angelo!' Mum had been shocked – embarrassed.

And when they had all gone out together for fish and chips, Mum and Rik had an argument about who would drive home. Then they both kept drinking until neither was fit to drive. They had to catch a bus and a train, at 10.30 p.m. and walk the last kilometre home from the station with Mum and Rik laughing all the way. By then they were really merry.

But Mum was furious the next day when, nursing her hangover, she had to catch the train and the bus back to the restaurant to pick up the car. They don't go out now. It's less hassle to stay at home. Mum and Rik drink as much as they want. Hellz keeps out of their way. There have been other 'Riks' in the last two years. Hellz hopes this one will not be around long either.

He opens the fridge. There is no Coke. Two six-packs of beer take up most of the top shelf. Damn! Mum hasn't done the shopping yet. She usually does it on the way home from work. Is that why she's home early? Hellz becomes conscious of the crystal again. It nudges his leg, niggling at him. He can't decide what to do with it. And he is desperately thirsty. He inspects the fridge. Not even any orange juice. And the tap water will be warm. He reaches in and slides one can out of the six pack. His mother doesn't let him drink alcohol. But he's so thirsty – and angry – he doesn't care.

Defiantly he takes the can outside, pulling the tab and listening to the hiss of the bubbles as he walks towards the garden shed. But he has forgotten the key for the padlock. He can't go back inside now. Not with an open can in his hand. He goes around to the back of the shed, out of sight of the house, and sits down. Leaning against the wall he swigs the cold, fizzy liquid. It tastes bitter, but refreshing. He takes another mouthful. This time it slides easily down his throat. His head begins to feel cool and light. The heavy, throbbing headache that has been hovering all day is gone.

He takes the crystal from his pocket but leaves it wrapped in the dried-out layers of toilet paper. He will bury it – in a minute.

As his body cools and relaxes, his anger shifts from Rik to his mother. Why does she need other people when he needs only her? Would she even miss him if he went away and never came back? Or if he died? He remembers the weird dream. The body, lying lifeless on the path. *His* body. His legs and arms spread wide. His hair across his face. And that Grim Reaper looking down.

'Just a dream,' Mum had said. But the Ancient Romans believed that dreams could predict the future. What if they were right?

Maybe he should sell the crystal, after all. Use the money to take off up north. Get a job on a station. He's tall enough and big for his age. He could tell them he's – maybe fifteen, or even seventeen. He wonders how much the shiny tear-drop is really worth.

As he swigs the last of the beer, he unwraps the crystal. Brightness leaps out at him as the sun bounces off the sharp angles. Hellz watches, mes-merised, his head swimming as a rainbow of colours streams away from the sparkling gem. He bends over it, trying to find the source of the rainbow. But his head blocks the sun, turning everything black and dead.

He lifts the crystal with two fingers and peers into its mysterious core. In spite of its clear outer brightness, there is a shadow at its centre that his eyes can't penetrate. As he lays the crystal back on the paper, the sun shines through it, concentrating its rays into a tiny circle of intense light. Fascinated, he moves the circle back and forth, like a torch beam on a wall. Then he holds it steady. Smoke begins to rise in curling spirals from the paper, as if the opaque centre of the crystal has, at last, escaped its glassy prison. The circle of light on the paper blackens and eats a smouldering hole right through to the sand below.

CHAPTER 13

Hellz forces himself to wake. His limbs are locked in position. His body is still gripped by panic even as his mind tells him it is only a dream. The same dream.

He hears Mum's voice.

'His school bag is inside the back door – as usual. But I haven't seen him all afternoon,' she says.

The door bangs. There are footsteps on the path.

'We could try the deli?' Tan says.

'He might be there,' Eddie replies, without much conviction. The voices fade as his head continues to spin.

Hellz's fingers are clamped tight around the crystal. When he opens his hand, the rainbow of the afternoon has been replaced by a pale, eerie evening light that pulses like a captured star.

He knows now that he can't bury it behind the shed. It will just keep calling, like the giant's harp in *Jack and the Beanstalk.* Calling to its owner. Or anyone who'll listen. He has a terrible feeling that he will never be free of its disturbing presence. A suffocating feeling spreads from his chest to his throat. His head aches. He struggles up. His legs feel dead. Pins and needles start to prickle behind his knees. He bends down to rub one leg and his shoulder hits the wall of the shed with a tinny clang.

'Is that you, Angelo?' He quickly slips the crystal back into his pocket. The fly screen door slams shut as Mum crosses the narrow strip of back lawn. 'What are you doing?'

'Nothin'.'

Mum gives him one of her piercing looks.

'Your mates were looking for you.'

'I had a lot of homework.'

'I looked in your room.'

'I came out for some air.'

'Well, dinner's ready.'

Back in the kitchen, Mum lifts the frothing pot

of pasta from the stove and drains off the water. She serves the succulent ribbons of fettuccini onto three plates, spoons the packet sauce over the top, and carries two of the plates through to the lounge room where the TV is blaring.

Hellz sits at the kitchen table and twists the pasta around his fork. He is ravenously hungry. But after a couple of mouthfuls he begins to feel ill again. He pushes his plate away.

Forgetting that there is no Coke, he opens the fridge. Rik comes in from the lounge room, staggering slightly, a stupid grin on his face. There is a strong smell of alcohol as Rik bends towards Hellz and looks past him, into the fridge.

'Where's my beer?' Rik demands. Hellz steps out of Rik's way, picks up his plate and puts it on the sink. Rik stares for a moment at the empty shelf then turns and grabs Hellz by the shoulder. 'I said *where's my beer*!' Hellz shrugs away from the grasping hand. The man goes to the doorway and shouts, 'Anna! Where's the rest of the beer?'

'It's gone,' she calls.

'It can't be!' Rik looks puzzled for a moment, then he rounds on Hellz.

'You been drinkin' it!' he says. 'You little weasel.

You have! You been drinkin' my beer!'

'Hey! Let go!' Hellz protests as the hand grabs his arm. He struggles and they both collide with a chair. It falls and Hellz trips over it. When he straightens his back there is a knife in Rik's hand.

The contorted face of Hellz's nightmare is now only centimetres from his own. Bloodshot eyes narrow theateningly. A steel-rope arm wraps tight around his neck. Instinctively Hellz turns his face away. The knife point is touching his cheek.

'No grubby, half-grown toad is gettin' away with drinkin' *my* beer. Y' hear me?' Hellz tries to nod. Rik sways unsteadily. For one split second a gap opens up between the knife and Hellz's cheek. Desperately, Hellz rams his elbow into the man's stomach. Doubling up, Rik loosens his grip. Hellz slips free and runs.

He is aware of his mother's stunned face in the doorway of the lounge room as he shoves through the back door and dashes down the path. He knows he must run. And he knows, even before he hears feet on the path behind him that Rik will follow.

'Come back here!' Rik bellows.

Hellz runs down the hill with the landscape of

his nightmare becoming terrifyingly real. He runs faster down the slope. But so does Rik. The beating footsteps keep pace with his own.

Hellz's breath burns in his lungs and his legs begin to tire. He stumbles, pushing his hand hard into his stomach, to ease the sharp pain of a stitch. He wants to stop. Turn back. Rewind the video. Anything to avoid going forward. But the dream holds him captive now. Even as he runs away, he knows he is running towards his own death.

Rik is just a couple of strides behind him. Catching up. The spaces close in. The darkness becomes more intense. If only Hellz could wake up. Sit up in bed. See the light coming in through his window and be safe in his own room in the morning. But he can't stop running.

The witch's fence looms in front of him. Her dog rushes out, barking, and baring its teeth. Hellz is fighting his fear. But he can't run any more. And there is nowhere else to hide.

When he reaches the gap between the bushes, he grips the top of the fence and flings his body up and over. He lands on all fours – right in the heart of the witch's den.

CHAPTER 14

Hellz tries not to think about the witch and her dog. The threat from Rik is more immediate. He scrambles up, gasping for air. At last, a breathing space, no matter how small. Then he looks down. The patterns of his nightmare are everywhere. The rough brick paving under his feet. The shadows. The Grim Reaper figure standing there. Black hood, pale, gaunt face, skeletal hand holding the oddly shaped scythe. Just a dream! He clings desperately to Mum's words.

His mind is blank; his body paralysed. A sound behind him starts his blood racing again. Before he can move, Rik is beside him. Hellz feels the steel grip around his neck. The knife against his face.

The black, silent figure in front of him stands

perfectly still. The dog circles all three of them, barking wildly. Rik kicks out at it with his foot, but does not connect.

Hellz struggles against the grip on his neck. But it tightens.

His chest, already heaving from the run down the hill, is about to explode. He fights to breathe. His eyes are streaming. The Grim Reaper steps towards him. The scythe is raised to strike him down. He turns his face away, digging his fingers desperately into the arm around his neck. The grip tightens even more. Hellz feels himself losing consciousness.

Then, from somewhere inside his nightmare, he hears a voice – scratchy with age, but full of anger.

'*Let him go!*'

'Stay out of this, you old bag of bones!' Rik snarls. His struggle with Hellz carries them both closer to Lallie. Light flashes on the curved silver handle as the walking stick comes down with a thwack.

The blow glances off Rik's shoulder. But he is so surprised by it that his grip slackens for an instant. Hellz breaks free and turns to run as Lallie steps between him and his attacker.

With her feet planted firmly on the path and her stick held up across her body with both hands, Lallie fends off the slashing knife that is now turned on her. She deflects several blows. Then, while Rik is off balance, she lifts her arm, draws it back and swings the stick deftly from her shoulder. It connects with a decisive thud, just below Rik's left ear. He drops to the ground.

Lallie stands over the fallen Rik. The light filtering through the bushes picks out her prominent bones, the black felt hat pulled down, like a hood, over her hair, the loose black gown and the distinctive stick with its curved silver handle. In the shadows, Hellz stands looking down on the body that lies on the paving, the straight brown hair almost covering the face, the long limbs spread-eagled. He sees, for the first time, the likeness between himself and Rik.

Mum is shouting. Running down the road. There is panic in her voice. But Hellz can't make out the words.

Two policemen appear at Lallie's gate. Mum barges past them. She rushes to Hellz and wraps him in her arms. Her grip is almost as tight as Rik's had been. But her words are loving and reassuring.

While one policeman bends over Rik, the other goes to Lallie.

'I'm all right,' she says, her voice shaking. 'Just give me a minute.' The policeman steadies her as she sits down on her stone step.

'Is this the man, Mrs Hellios?' The policeman rolls Rik onto his side. He splutters and opens his eyes. Hellz's mum nods and turns away.

'Bitch!' Rik spits the word at her. He struggles to his feet, but both policemen have hold of him.

Mum jerks around to face him. 'You're a maniac!' she shouts, still clinging protectively to Hellz. 'Don't you *ever* come near us again!'

Rik is still hurling abuse as the policemen shove him into their car.

Hellz digs into his pocket. Slipping free of his mother's embrace, he holds the crystal out to Lallie. The lines of age and weariness fall away from her face and she smiles up at him.

'I'm sorry,' Hellz says. The crystal splashes reflected light in her eyes before her hand closes over it.

'Thank you,' she says softly.

CHAPTER 15

Lallie wakes feeling slow and heavy. The events of last night come flooding back as she tries to move her aching legs. The dog gets up and stands beside her bed. She looks at him and laughs.

'Winston, will you take off that gloomy face?' she says. 'I know I look like a close relative of Doctor Death, but I *am* still alive. Nothing is broken *and* our crystal has come back to us. So let's celebrate.'

She limps in to her kitchen and fills the kettle. Lifting the lid off the small compost bucket on her bench, she tips in the cold tea leaves from her infuser. The bucket is full. She decides to empty it into the compost bin in her garden while she waits for the water to boil.

Lallie opens her back door, but stops, stunned, in the doorway.

She covers her eyes, unable to believe what she sees, hoping that when she looks again, everything will be as it was. But when she does look, her worst fears are confirmed.

It's as if a herd of elephants has charged through her garden during the night. Plants lie flattened, their leaves bruised and scattered. Yellow heads of chamomile are squashed into the churned black soil. A broken branch swings like a fractured limb from one side of the lemon tree. Lallie feels as shocked and wounded as if she herself had been trampled.

Who could have done this? Those kids again? She pictures Hellz's face as he handed her the crystal. 'No. Not him. Not last night,' she muses. 'But the others wouldn't do it without their leader, would they, Winston?' she asks. The dog is also looking at the garden. Her hand goes down to stroke his neck. 'Then again, if it's not the kids, who is it? Who would do such a wickedly destructive thing.' She walks despondently among the broken stems and squashed leaves, still carrying her bucket of kitchen scraps.

The compost bin, when she reaches it, is lying on its side, its contents scattered. The colony of earthworms, usually crawling all over the dark inside walls of the bin, are nowhere to be seen.

Lallie lifts the hollow plastic barrel and begins to scrape the scattered debris into a pile. Winston snuffles at the partly decomposed food scraps and follows his nose across the flattened garden to the fence. Lallie sees him concentrating on something there and goes to investigate. Two footprints, side by side, are pressed into the soft earth. Someone has swung over her back fence. Lallie immediately pictures Hellz coming over her front fence and landing in exactly that way.

'But why, Winston?' She is completely baffled. 'Youthful high spirits? I vaguely remember suffering from them myself, way back in the dawn of time. But I would not have dreamed of doing something like this ...' She shakes her head sorrowfully.

Looking closely at the footprints, Lallie sees that they match the one she has already recorded. Hellz would be big enough to wear sneakers of that size. His two mates are smaller. But she can't think of anyone else who wears sneakers.

'Anyway, you're supposed to warn me when strangers are in the yard.' Winston looks up at her.

'You're not going to tell me it *wasn't* a stranger.' She pushes the idea away and stands, glaring down at the footprints, willing them to reveal the identity of their owner.

Anxious and unsure of what to do next, the dog sits down – on top of the footprints. 'Winston!' Lallie cries. 'Now you've destroyed the evidence.' Winston gets to his feet and stands with his stump of a tail tucked in. 'Oh, never mind. The police will only laugh at me again. They'll tell me I can't prove it. But I'm *sure* they are the same footprints as last time.'

CHAPTER 16

'Hellz!' Tan shouts and runs to catch up with him. Hellz does not slacken his pace and Tan has to do little skips every so often to keep up with him. 'We been lookin' for ya, Eddie and me.'

'I been busy,' Hellz says coolly.

'Hey man, we *really* got that old witch back.' Tan thumps one fist into the palm of his other hand. 'How much did ya get for the crystal?'

'Nuthin'.'

Tan looks puzzled. 'Why?'

'I didn't sell it.'

Tan's face clears. 'Good thinkin', Hellz. Wait 'til the cops have forgotten about it, eh? Where'd ya hide it?'

'I gave it back.'

'*What*?'

Hellz's dark eyes look steadily at Tan, but he doesn't repeat the words. Tan begins to laugh.

'Very funny, Hellz,' he says. When the expression on Hellz's face doesn't change, Tan becomes angry. 'Whadda y' mean, y' *gave it back.* Eddie and me helped nick that crystal. *We* got a right to our share o' the cash.'

'Forget it!' Hellz says vehemently. 'It wasn't worth anythin' in the end. Just an old bit of glass.'

'Aw, come on. I never seen glass like that before. All those colours. And the spiral bit in the centre. You sold it. Didn' ya! You sold it and now you're gunna keep *all* the money!' Tan's sallow face flushes and his wiry frame jerks with pent-up energy. He scowls and pushes Hellz's shoulder with his hand. Hellz grabs the front of Tan's shirt and glares at him. But Tan shouts into his face. 'Think you're big time, don't ya! Well, you're *not*! You're just a sneaky, cheatin' little *maggot*!'

Hellz suddenly lets go of Tan, spins away and walks off, very fast. Beneath his long strides, the familiar pavement passes like a conveyor belt. Around the corner he begins to run. When he reaches the bottom of his own driveway, the memory of the previous afternoon stops him in his tracks. He walks cautiously towards the house even though he knows that Rik is still in custody, trying to raise bail.

Carefully Hellz opens the door. The house is cool and still and quiet. He lets his bag thump onto the kitchen floor.

In the fridge he finds a cold sausage. He lifts it off the plate. It brings two fins of congealed fat with it. Hellz eats the whole lot then takes his skateboard out onto the street.

Thick curling ropes of grey cloud fill up the sky. The wind swirls and pushes them upwards as if the lid has just been lifted off the cauldron of the world.

Hellz waits beside the fence in the usual meeting place. He knows Tan won't show. But there's no sign of Eddie, either. He pictures Tan going on about the crystal, giving Eddie an earful. *So what?* he says to himself. Tan has been getting too pushy lately, anyway. He misses Eddie though.

While he's standing there, his eyes are drawn to the bushy fence line of Lallie's house at the bottom of the street. Then he is walking down the hill.

He hesitates in front of her gate. As he pushes

it open, Winston confronts him. But he doesn't bark. His head is on one side and his eyes are curious. Hellz bends down and gives him a pat.

Lallie rises silently from her usual chair on the veranda, but she doesn't come towards him. Her eyes rove warily around and behind him.

'Where are your friends?' Lallie asks.

Hellz shrugs. He doesn't even know why *he* is standing on her front path, much less where the others are.

'Come,' the old woman says. Hellz is not known for his obedience, but this time he follows, drawn by curiosity and a new respect for his former enemy.

Lallie leads him around the side of the house. Winston patrols behind them. When the back garden comes into view they all stop.

Still unable to fully comprehend the destruction of her precious plants, Lallie stands, shaking her head. She turns to Hellz and studies him carefully. Hellz feels her eyes reaching into him. Turning him inside out.

'What happened?' he says at last.

'I'm glad you asked,' Lallie finally looks away. 'I can see, now, that you didn't do it. But, make no mistake, I'll find out who did. And when I do . . .'

CHAPTER 17

The phone rings inside the house. Lallie hobbles in through the back door calling, 'Come on in. Have some cake.' Winston trots after her.

Hellz hovers outside the door. The smell of warm cake wafts towards him. He looks into the kitchen. Ancient, leather-bound books are piled up on one end of the table. Strings of garlic and chilli peppers hang down like Christmas decorations on either side of the wood-burning stove. A huge, earthenware cauldron with a wooden tap at the bottom dominates a low bench in the pantry that opens off the far side of the room. All the things Hellz has heard about the old woman race through his mind. He turns to go.

'No!' Lallie says fiercely. Hellz stops. Then he realises that she is not talking to him. 'I am *not* selling my house! Ever!' She slams down the phone. 'Estate agents!' she says, exasperated. 'They really are the lowest form of life!'

'Come in.' She beckons to Hellz. He steps into the kitchen. On the other side of the room the open window looks out onto the street. A familiar shaft of rainbow light slices through the dimness and comes to rest on the floor at his feet. The clouds have shifted. The sun shines through the crystal. Hanging once more from its piece of fishing line, it turns slowly in the breeze. The finger of light seems to follow Hellz as he moves towards the table.

Lallie pulls out a chair. Hellz sits down slowly, his back to the window. A warm glow travels up his leg and comes to rest on his shoulder, as the shaft of light spins and settles itself again. He is conscious of the gentle warmth. So different from the searing heat that the crystal gave off when he carried it in his pocket. There are questions he wants to ask about this. But not yet. He is not ready to remind Lallie that he stole it.

'You're Hellz, aren't you?'

Hellz is surprised. How does she know his name? He remembers Eddie saying that you must never let a witch know your name. It gives them power over you. He feels that power tugging at him and struggles against it. 'It's an unusual name,' Lallie says. 'How do you spell it?' Hellz hesitates.

'A-n-g-e-l-o,' he says slowly. The tugging eases.

'Ah,' Lallie replies, nodding. 'But you're no angel.' She grins at him and the power balances out. He grins back.

Hellz looks around the room. Opposite where he is sitting, among the woven wall hangings and carved wooden figurines, he sees a faded photograph in a frame. It shows two people astride a 1950s Harley Davidson. The rider is taller and more solid than the passenger. Both are wearing jeans and leather jackets, their heads encased in heavy, old-fashioned helmets.

Hellz leans forward, examining the picture. 'Nice Harley,' he says as Lallie places a patterned china plate in front of him.

'You know about Harleys, do you?' she asks.

'They're the best,' he says. 'Is that your husband?' He points to the figure on the front of the bike.

Lallie laughs. 'Good heavens, no,' she says. 'Even if I *had* agreed to marry the father of my child, I wouldn't have trusted him to ride *my* Harley!' She reaches over and lifts the picture from the wall. 'That's me!' she says. 'And that's my son, Herman, on the back. We went everywhere on that bike. Just loaded up the saddle bags and took off, in those days.'

Lallie cuts three wedges of fluffy yellow cake. She places one on the plate in front of Hellz. Soft white icing bulges at the top of the slice. Winston sits beside Lallie, gazing up into her face.

'It's not good for your teeth, Winston,' she warns, then hands him the biggest wedge. Long, sharp teeth close over the delicious morsel. Hellz is glad his fingers are well away.

There is silence in the kitchen while they all eat. Then Hellz swallows and asks, 'Did you get a lot of money when you sold your Harley?'

'I could never sell it,' Lallie says. 'I don't ride it now, of course. I don't want to lose the use of my legs, so I walk most places. But I still have Priscilla – in the back shed.' Hellz's eyes widen and he almost chokes on the last crumb of cake. 'Would you like to see her?' Lallie asks.

Nodding enthusiastically, Hellz follows Lallie out into the backyard. They walk along the rough pathway beside the flattened garden. The old wooden shed is completely hidden by creepers and vines, except for a small window, covered in cobwebs. Murmuring endearments, Lallie peers into one corner of the window. Apparently satisfied with what she sees, she repeats the same sounds three times, peering in turn at the other corners. The sounds become a kind of chant. Hellz imagines the rickety door opening by magic to this incantation.

'Just checking my babies,' Lallie explains. She gives the door a hefty shove and it creaks open. 'Very useful creatures, spiders. Don't know what I would do without them. They kill off all sorts of nasty bugs that would otherwise eat my . . .' she glances back at the wreckage, '. . . my beautiful garden,' she says sadly. But Hellz's eyes are focused on the shape beneath the dusty canvas cover.

Lallie pulls away the shroud. Dust billows up into the roof space of the small shed. Lallie coughs, flaps at the cloud with her free hand and flings the cover out through the door. Hellz stands reverently beside the gleaming flanks of the motorcycle. Lallie watches him closely.

'Hop on,' she says. 'Try her out. I've drained the petrol, of course. But you can still get the feel of her.'

Hellz hesitates, but Lallie encourages him with a nod of her head. With the biggest smile Lallie has seen on anyone for a long time, Hellz climbs aboard the Harley.

In seconds he is transported to the open road. He imagines the wheels bouncing slightly as they come down off the double stand, the engine springing to life with a throaty growl. He feels the weight of the helmet on his head, the wind against his body as he leans the powerful machine into a corner.

When Hellz becomes conscious of his surroundings again, Lallie is watching him.

'What's your son's name?' Hellz asks her.

'Herman.'

'Why doesn't *he* ride Priscilla?'

'Saints preserve us!' Lallie gives one of her spluttering cackles. 'Hopeless, is why! Just like his father. Poor boy.' She pauses for a moment, suddenly serious, then asks, 'What about *your* father?' Hellz looks puzzled. 'They're keeping him in custody, I believe.'

Now it's Hellz's turn to splutter. 'He's not my father! No way!'

'Oh,' Lallie says. 'You look alike. At least I

thought so.' She turns away, curious, but not wanting to pry. She steps outside the door and drags the canvas cover back in. There is a long silence. Hellz gets down from the Harley.

'My father died two years ago.' The words struggle out of him.

'I'm sorry,' Lallie says.

'He crashed his Harley.' Hellz wipes his hand across his nose. 'Mum wanted him to sell it. She hated it. But he was always careful when *I* was on the back.'

'Where were you that day?'

'At a party. I shouldn't have gone. It was just a kid from school. I didn't even like him much . . . If I'd stayed with Dad . . .' Hellz gulps and swallows. 'We were mates,' he adds.

'And you've been in trouble ever since,' Lallie says quietly. Hellz looks straight ahead, then squeezes his eyes closed.

They replace the cover and close up the shed in silence. As they walk back down the path, Lallie stoops to gather up several fallen lemons.

'At least the fruit is not ruined,' she says. 'Would your mother like these?'

Hellz shakes his head. 'She doesn't have time to make cake,' he says.

'No,' Lallie says pensively. 'I dare say she doesn't. I fear I may have misjudged your mother.' She absentmindedly brushes the sand off the rough yellow skins. Then her face brightens. 'You can squeeze lemon juice on to your fish, you know. When you have fish and chips. You *do* eat fish and chips?' she raises one eyebrow at Hellz. He grins. There is nothing funny about fish and chips. But suddenly he feels like laughing.

They walk back to the house together. 'You haven't told me where your friends are this afternoon,' Lallie reminds him. Hellz gives that same shrug of his shoulders that Lallie is coming to recognise.

'They weren't with *you* last night,' she probes. 'Is it possible that they were doing elephant impersonations in my garden?'

'No! Well, I don't know.' Hellz is confused. 'I don't think so.'

It hadn't occurred to him. But now he can't be sure. Maybe Tan trashed Lallie's garden to big-note himself. Show he could do stuff on his own. Hellz is suddenly angry. Angry and suspicious.

'I'll find out,' he says. 'Thanks for the Harley ride – and the cake,' he calls, and runs down the side path.

'See you later,' Lallie says softly.

CHAPTER 18

Tan's father is in the garden when Hellz arrives.

'What you want?' he says. 'You make trouble for Tan.'

'I want to ask him something.'

'He not here.'

'Where, then?'

'Go away.'

On the way home, Hellz calls at Eddie's house. There is no one there.

Mum leaves the television when she hears him in the kitchen.

'Are you okay?' she asks.

'Yeah,' Hellz lies.

'It's just ... well ... your skateboard was outside ... but you weren't.'

'I decided to take the Rolls out for a spin instead.'

Hellz puts on a plummy voice, waving an imaginary cigarette holder and swaggering across the room.

'I was worried,' Mum says.

Hellz stops. Suddenly his mother looks smaller, older. 'Sorry,' he says, giving her a lopsided grin. Her face clears and she smiles at him.

Hellz finally spots Tan the next day, on the other side of the school basketball court. Weaving between the kids and dodging loose balls, he makes his way across.

But by the time he reaches the other side, Tan has disappeared. Hellz looks around. He catches sight of Eddie a hundred metres away, in the undercover area. He can't be sure that she has *deliberately* turned her back. So he walks slowly towards her. Her friends are still there when he arrives, but Eddie has gone.

'Where'd Eddie go?' he asks Emma. The girls in the group exchange glances and giggle.

'She's not talking to you.'

'Why?' he asks, but they run off.

Hellz shrugs and turns away. But there is an emptiness inside him. He is surprised by the hurt, the feeling of betrayal. It's as if he's been numb for a long time. Now, suddenly he wants to belong.

For the rest of the day Hellz plays it cool, but keeps his eyes open. Eddie is not in any of the usual places. And Tan is definitely avoiding him.

The minute his class is dismissed, Hellz grabs his bag and runs to the door of Tan's classroom, dodging a mother and a little kid on the path. Tan is just coming out. He sees Hellz, but tries to push past him. Hellz grabs his arm.

'Wait.'

Tan tries to pull away.

'What've you been sayin' to Eddie?'

'Nothin'.'

'Oh yeah?'

'I don't want to talk to you.'

'Just listen then.'

'Why should I?'

'Did *you* do the witch's garden?'

'What?'

'The garden. Did you *do* it?'

'Get lost!' Tan swings his school bag at Hellz. Hellz catches it, jerks it. The two boys wrestle each other to the ground. For all his smaller size, Tan is tenacious. Kids from his class try to drag them apart. Then Tan's teacher appears in the doorway.

'Stop that this minute! Both of you!' she calls.

They get up. Tan straightens his clothes, glaring at Hellz, and starts to walk away.

'No, wait! Please!'

There is an urgency in Hellz's voice that surprises Tan. He stops and turns around.

'Look, I know you think I cheated you with the crystal,' Hellz says, striding towards Tan.

'You did!'

'But Lallie . . .'

'Who?'

'Lallie . . . Mrs Hagbert . . . the *witch. You* know.' Hellz is talking as fast as he can. He knows Tan will not listen for long. 'Anyway she . . .' he stops. 'Let's go along the drain,' he says. He needs more time to form the words. And he wants to look at the water. He knows it will be flowing, calm and clear, between its high, grassy banks. More like a stream than a drain, it always has a soothing effect on Hellz. Tan kicks defiantly at a stone, but leaves the path and walks with him towards the trees that line the banks.

Looking down on the slow-moving water, Tan stops, picks up a stick and throws it in. Both boys watch it travel down the stream, crash into the bank, swirl away again and disappear from sight.

'I really did give it back,' Hellz says at last.

Tan looks at him. 'Liar!' he says.

'She saved my life,' Hellz says softly. 'And I gave her crystal back.'

Tan stares at Hellz.

'Saved your life? She must be ninety! How come *she* saved *your* life?'

'Rik came after me with a knife.'

'Jeez, Hellz, y' must have made him real mad.' A grudging admiration creeps into Tan's voice.

'I drank his beer.'

'Drank his beer!' The admiration increases. 'But where did he get the knife?'

'I didn't ask him. I just ran.'

'Bet you broke the Olympic record. But how come that old witch helped you out? She hates you. She hates all of us.'

'She was great.' Hellz feels his shoulders curling inwards at the memory of it. 'I'm runnin'. Rik is right behind me. This close.' He indicates with his hands. 'He's a crazy drunk and he's gunna kill me! I see her bushes. There's nowhere else to hide. I jump the fence but she's right there with that walking stick of hers. She lifts it up.' Hellz demonstrates. 'I think she's going to belt me with it. Next minute she's using it to fend off Rik – and the knife.'

'Jeez,' Tan says again.

'It's funny, though,' Hellz says.

'Sounds dead serious to me.'

'No. Not that.' Hellz picks up a stone and adjusts the bag on his back. 'I did the graffiti, right?' He throws the stone into the drain. Tan gives Hellz a curious look, but nods his head.

'And the crystal.'

'No! *We* did the crystal.'

Tan is sounding tetchy again so Hellz goes on quickly, 'Then, last night, someone trashes her garden.' Tan looks puzzled. Hellz leans his face in close to Tan. 'Well?' he asks.

'What? She's blamin' *us* for it?'

'She knows *I* didn't do it,' Hellz says.

'Well don't look at me!' Tan is indignant.

'Who, then?' Hellz asks. Tan shrugs. 'She's pretty upset,' Hellz continues, 'says she'll have to call the cops. And y' know what *they'll* say.'

'That's not fair!' Tan splutters. 'My old man will go right off his trolley if the cops show up at our place again.'

'Yeah, but . . . if we can find out who really did it . . .' Hellz says persuasively. Tan is not listening.

'Where does that old bag get off? I'm not gunna be hauled off to the cop shop *again* for somethin' I didn't even do!' He marches angrily away.

'Where y' goin'?' Hellz asks.

'Where d' y' think?' Tan calls back at him. 'I'm gunna *tell* her!'

Hellz tries to keep the smile from showing on his face as he catches up to Tan.

CHAPTER 19

They find Lallie sitting beside her ruined garden. Her shoulders are slumped. At first she doesn't see them. She is saying something. To herself. A chant, or a poem maybe. Hellz thinks it's the saddest thing he has ever heard.

. . . never an hour is fair wi' flower,
And never a flower wi' dew.

When she does look up at them her eyes are damp but smouldering.

'I haven't made cake today,' she says despondently, looking from Hellz to Tan. 'But there are biscuits.'

'We've come to help,' Hellz says.

Lallie looks surprised. 'How kind. And what an asset, being able to cook at your age,' she says.

'Not with the cake,' Hellz says. 'Tan and me, well we thought we could help you find out who did it. You know, take turns to watch the house, or somethin'.'

'Oh,' Lallie hesitates. 'Well . . . I don't know . . .' she begins, turning the idea over in her head. 'Yes! Why not? I'll let your parents – and the police – know that you are helping me. We can do three shifts.' She takes off her hat and shakes her wayward hair loose. 'But what about your school work? You'll be too tired. It happens at night, you know.'

'This is our last week,' Hellz says.

Lallie looks thoughtful again. 'What about your other friend?'

'Eddie's not allowed to hang out with us any more,' Tan says. Hellz receives this news like a blow to his body.

'Oh?' Lallie says, looking at Hellz.

'They're leavin' early for their holidays,' Tan continues importantly. 'And they're sellin' their house.'

'Why would they want to sell such a grand house?' Lallie asks.

'Eddie's folks reckon this neighbourhood is gettin' too rough.'

Hellz is looking more and more agitated. 'Ah, sorry,' he says. 'I have to go.'

Lallie looks into him in that way she has. 'Yes,' she says. 'I can see you do. Never mind. I'll think about your offer. Come back tomorrow – if you haven't changed your mind.' She calls the last part of the sentence after him as he runs down the path. Tan follows.

'I can't believe you dobbed us in for helpin' the old witch!' Tan runs across the road to catch up with Hellz. A car coming down the hill narrowly misses him. The driver blasts his horn. Tan whirls around, making a defiant gesture with two fingers. When he is beside Hellz he says, 'You gone soft or somethin'?'

'She's okay,' Hellz says, striding towards Eddie's gate. 'Tough and . . .' he pauses, searching for a word, 'gritty.'

'Yeah, gritty. Like sandpaper – she wears ya down!'

Hellz isn't listening.

There is one car in Eddie's double driveway. The two boys walk up the path and Hellz presses the bell. In spite of small sounds from inside the house, no one opens the door.

Hellz presses the bell again. This time there is complete silence.

'Not home,' Tan says.

Hellz is not so sure. He turns away from the door just in time to see the curtain fall back at the front window.

As they go out through the gate, Tan says, 'I told you.'

'What?' Hellz glares at Tan. He wants to grab hold of him and shake him. But somehow he doesn't have the energy.

'Her dad won't let her talk to you any more. Since Rik and the cops and everythin'. That's why they're goin' on their holidays early. And she's goin' to St Mary's next year.'

'St Mary's! She'll hate it!' Moving house is bad news. But St Mary's! He won't even get to see Eddie at school.

'Her dad reckons she'll make the right kind of friends there,' Tan says.

'Yeah, the boring kind,' Hellz snaps.

Hoping Tan has got it all wrong, Hellz checks with Emma when he gets to school in the morning. It's true. Eddie is leaving. It's her last day.

Hellz still can't find her. She's deliberately avoiding him. It's not her style, but hey . . . The world has tipped upside down and nothing is the same as it used to be. Maybe she's embarrassed about this thing with her dad. Or is that just an excuse and the truth is she doesn't like him any more. He needs to talk to her. Tell her things he should have told her before. As usual, he's made a mess of everything.

Hellz slouches miserably along the path. He's been everywhere. There's nowhere else to go. His head is down, shoes scuffing the bitumen. Several kids run past. They jostle him. He ignores them. Then three little kids come careering around the corner of the lunch shed.

There'll never be enough room for all four of them between the shed and the classroom. The first kid crashes into Hellz. The other two crash into both of them. The first kid's nose starts bleeding. Blood goes everywhere. The other kids start bawling. Hellz is shoved hard up against a rubbish bin. It's the suspended type, strapped to a pole. The strap chooses that precise moment in its long and useful life to develop a stress fracture and – crash!

The full bin falls and tips on its side. The lid flies off, emptying lunch scraps all over Hellz and the little kids. Splattered with blood, tomato sauce and sticky wrappers, Hellz towers over the tangled, blubbering bodies. The smell is appalling.

A crowd comes from nowhere, expanding like a mushroom cloud. Within seconds the whole school is there, watching, doubling up with contagious laughter. Hellz closes his eyes. For the first time in his whole life he wishes he *was* an angel. Then he could take off. Fly up to heaven. Or anywhere. Just as far away from here as possible.

Back in class there is an uneasy silence.

'I believe you have just demolished a bin and mown down three Year Ones in one fell swoop, Mr Hellios. That is pretty spectacular, even for you.' Mr Sharp inspects him closely, then turns his head away to escape the smell. Hellz stands, head down, saying nothing. Mr Sharp waits.

'Have you nothing to say in your defence?' he asks. Hellz doesn't move. 'Did anyone else see this unfortunate incident? Anyone who can *reliably* tell us exactly what happened?' Mr Sharp asks the class. Silence.

'Come on, class.' Mr Sharp is getting impatient. 'We have one broken nose, a collection of grazes and bruises and a path bearing a striking resemblance to a Jackson Pollock painting.' He strides to the window and stands looking out towards the devastation. A few kids begin to titter behind their hands.

Mr Sharp spins back to face them and the noise abates. But no one speaks up for Hellz. This time it is *not* his fault and they know it. But there is only silence.

'Yes,' Mr Sharp swings his finger in the general direction of the earlier sounds. He points to Stephen Oliver. 'You have something to say?' Stephen ducks and leaves the finger pointing at the girl behind him. 'If I don't get a response from someone, you will *all* be out there cleaning up the mess.'

'They were running,' the girl says.

'Ah. Now we're getting to it. Is this true, Hellios?' Hellz feels Mr Sharp's eyes on him. He doesn't know why he can't seem to say anything. Normally he would have given them all a piece of his mind. Whatever he says they'll think it was his fault. But that wouldn't have stopped him in the past.

'All right. Running on the path. Deliberately breaking a school rule and endangering other students. Go to the registrar. Ask for a bucket and scrubbing brush from the cleaner's store and get that mess cleaned up. We will talk about *setting a good example to people younger than oneself* at a later time.'

On his hands and knees, nauseated by the smell of the rubbish and the smell of his own clothes, Hellz tries to summon up his old anger. But he just feels a flat helplessness. It's not his fault that little kids *run* everywhere. What's he supposed to do? Stand there all day like a cop directing traffic? Lecture them about not running? Some kids have to run.

He is conscious of the classroom window, looking out onto the path beside the lunch shed. And the kids coming and going. Laughing at him. Here's another one. Come to gloat. He won't look up.

He keeps scrubbing. The person on the path in front of him doesn't move. He's thinking *Get lost, will ya*! Then he recognises the sneakers. Only one kid in the school gets away with wearing shoes like that. He looks up slowly. Eddie!

'Hey,' she grins down at him. 'Specky pavement art.' He gives her the widest smile he can manage. 'I came to give you a hand.'

'Cool. I can use one – or ten. But won't you be in trouble with Mrs Thing?'

'Mrs Tring, Hellz.'

'That's right, Tring-a-ling.'

Eddie laughs at his bicycle-bell impersonation. Then she shakes her head. 'It's my last day,' she says sadly. 'Mrs Tring figures she doesn't have to be responsible for me actually learning anything today, so she might as well get me out of her classroom. Kids kept comin' in, laughin' and sayin, "*ew gross!*" So I put up me hand.

'"What is it, Edwina", she says. 'Y' know how she talks.' Hellz nods. 'Then I say, "It's not fair. The Year Ones should have to help." She says that the one with the broken nose is in hospital and the others have gone home. Everyone starts laughin' again, so I say "I'm gunna help then." Y'shoulda seen them. Stunned or what?'

Now it's Hellz who laughs. Picturing Eddie, socking it to the class. Happy that she is still his friend and just enjoying her being there.

They work for a while, side by side. Hellz scrubs

and Eddie sloshes water from the bucket wherever he needs it. Finally Eddie drags a hose from around the corner to get rid of the last of the mess.

'Watch out!' she calls. 'I'm the Wicked Witch of Hastings Street,' and she squirts Hellz with the hose.

'Hey!' he begins to protest. But the water is cool against his skin as it washes the blood, and the smell, out of his clothes. Hellz stands on the grass, arms stretched out, head thrown back, laughing while Eddie hoses him down.

More faces appear at the windows.

'Look at those wimps,' Eddie says. She swings the hose in their direction. Water rattles loudly against the glass and the faces flinch and blur.

Hellz, still laughing, thumbs his nose at them.

At last Eddie turns the hose off and they sit on a bench to dry out.

'I wish you didn't have to go,' Hellz says.

'Yeah,' Eddie agrees. 'It's a real bummer. I've been fightin' with Dad for a week, but he won't budge. Mum says we'll see what happens after the holidays, but they've put the house on the market and Mrs Tring is sendin' my stuff on to St Mary's.'

All the laughter has dried up in Hellz. 'Can you come skateboarding after school?'

'Sorry, Mum's got the car packed, ready. We have to go straight away and pick up Dad.' Eddie looks at him. 'Hey, it'll be okay. I'll write. And I'll ring you when we get back, yeah?'

'Promise?'

'Cross my heart . . . and have to fly.' She turns her head to acknowledge the kid from her class who has come to fetch her back inside. 'See ya.'

'See ya, Eddie.'

Hellz stays on the bench, drying off. Feeling sad and happy at the same time.

After school, Hellz stops in at home and changes his clothes. Tan slouches in the bedroom doorway, waiting.

'You really gunna do this detective thing?' he asks. Hellz nods. 'Checkin' out her valuables, eh?'

'Get outta here!' Hellz is furious.

'Ah, there you are.' Lallie greets them at the door.

'Did you talk to your friend?'

Hellz nods.

'Is everything okay?'

'No. She has to go. Her dad says.'

'But you are still friends.'

'Yes.'

'Good.' She ushers them inside.

Lallie puts cake and lemonade on the table.

They talk through several plans and agree to run them by Hellz's mum first. It's getting late, so Tan goes on home.

Lallie and Hellz approach his front door together. Lallie carries a freshly baked lemon cake.

'Mum!' Hellz opens the door and shouts down the passageway.

'Yes?' The voice is raised above the level of the TV.

Hellz stands with Lallie in the doorway to the lounge room. Eventually Mum turns around.

'Oh,' she says, lifting herself out of her chair. 'What's he done this time?'

'Hellz and Tan have offered to help me track down some villains,' Lallie says, ignoring the question. 'With your permission, of course.'

'What villains?' Mum asks. 'I don't want Angelo anywhere *near* any villains. He gets into enough trouble on his own.'

'I understand your concern, Mrs Hellios.'

'I doubt it,' Mum says. Then her face softens. 'Look, I really am grateful for what you did the other night, but . . .'

Lallie holds up her hand. 'No, please, hear me out. The boys will be perfectly safe. And I think it will be a valuable learning experience for them,' Lallie says. She raises her eyebrows and gives Mum a wink.

'Mmm,' Mum says thoughtfully. 'Set a thief to catch a thief?'

'Precisely,' Lallie replies.

'What?' Hellz leans in to hear what they say.

'Could we discuss this over a cup of tea?' Lallie asks.

'Good idea,' Mum says.

Once the two women get chatting, there seems to be no stopping them. Hellz takes his skateboard and leaves them to it.

Eventually Mum and Lallie go together to Tan's house. Tan's parents take more persuading, but they finally agree to a trial run. Tan and Hellz will help Lallie keep watch each night for a week. If they haven't discovered anything in that time, they will abandon the plan. But everyone agrees it's worth a try.

In Lallie's herb-scented kitchen, she and the two boys sit down to discuss the details.

'And straight against that great array,
Forth went the dauntless three . . .'

Lallie chants, sipping her tea.

'It's *third* for three, not *fourth,*' Tan says, pouring more lemonade into his glass.

'What's dauntless?' Hellz asks.

Lallie laughs. 'It's a poem,' she says. 'To stir the blood before going into battle. Dauntless means brave.'

'Why don't they write it in English?' Tan wants to know.

'It's Old English,' Lallie says. 'Although the story was probably first told in Latin – or maybe Italian,' she muses. Both boys are looking at her expectantly, so she continues. 'The Roman army had been driven back by the Tuscans until the only hope of saving the city of Rome was to chop down the last remaining bridge and stop the Tuscans crossing the river. But it was a solid bridge and they were never going to be able to chop it down in time. So Horatius asked for two volunteers to stand on the bridge with him and take on any Tuscans who tried to cross. Delaying tactics. You know?

> *'In yon straight path a thousand may well be*
> *stopped by three.*

Now who will stand on either hand and keep
the bridge with me?

Tan leans towards Hellz, 'What's she sayin'?' he asks. Hellz ignores him.

'Imagine. Standing there, on the bridge, with the whole Tuscan army coming at you, and your own soldiers hacking away underneath,' Lallie continues. 'No wonder Roman mothers prayed for –

Boys with hearts as bold
As his who kept the bridge so well
In the brave days of old.'

'What happened?' Hellz asks when Lallie falls silent.

'As the bridge fell, the other two managed to scramble back to their own side, but Horatius had further to go.'

'Did they kill him?' Tan asks.

'He dived into the river,' Lallie says. 'But he was still wearing all his armour. And, earlier, he'd been wounded in the thigh by one of the Tuscans.'

'So he drowned, then,' Hellz says sadly.

'Everyone thought he would drown,' Lallie replies. 'There was hardly a sound from either side of the river as he struggled and sank. But then they saw the plumes of his helmet rise above the surface. The Romans all started cheering like mad. Even the Tuscans could not remain silent.

'But his limbs were borne up bravely by the brave heart within.
'Curse on him' quoth false Sextus. 'Will not the villain drown?'
'Heaven help him' quoth Lars Porsena. 'And bring him safe to shore;
For such a gallant feat of arms was never seen before.'

The two boys sit, staring at Lallie.

'Lars Porsena was a Tuscan and false Sextus was a Roman traitor, fighting *with* the Tuscans,' she says.

'Yeah, but . . .'

'What happened to Horatius?'

'Oh, he made it to the shore and the Romans carried him in triumph through the city gates, and Lord Macaulay wrote a poem about him,' Lallie explains. 'Now, enough of the brave days of old, we've got our *own* battle to plan!'

Everyone wants to do the first shift. After several arguments they agree to draw straws at the beginning of each night's watch and do two-hour stints from 10 p.m. to first light.

They do not have long to wait. Hellz is just changing places with Lallie at midnight, when a hail of stones hits her bedroom window. Winston leaps up, ears pricked and tail high. Lallie catches hold of his collar as Hellz slips silently out of the back door with Lallie's camera in his hand.

'Get out of here!' Lallie shouts, moving her curtain aside and adding her voice to Winston's deep-throated growls. 'What sort of coward picks on an old woman living alone?' she calls out loudly to cover any noise that Hellz might be making as he races out the back way to try and photograph the culprit. 'You lily-livered worm! You half-baked fruit-cake! Or is it fruit-loop?' She pauses for breath. 'You yellow-bellied, pea-brained, disgustingly slimy *snake*!'

A car starts up from the other side of the fence and roars away. Tan emerges from his camp bed, staggering a little under the weight of interrupted sleep, just as Hellz comes back.

'Did you get the pictures?' Lallie says. Her cheeks are flushed and her eyes are dancing.

'I took one of him running – but he was in the shadows by then,' he says.

'Oh no!' Lallie sits down on the nearest chair. 'Don't tell me you missed him.'

'Well, yes,' Hellz admits. 'But I got a great shot of the car.'

'Good lad!' Lallie's face brightens and she almost leaps from the chair. 'I already have photos of the damage to the garden. We'll get this film developed first thing in the morning. *Then* we shall see what we shall see.'

CHAPTER

They sit around the table in Lallie's kitchen, studying the photos.

'This can't be the right film,' she says, looking up at Hellz.

'Yeah,' Hellz assures her. 'These are the shots I took. Y' can just see someone running. It's a bit dark, but y' can see the outline and the light-coloured sneakers. This is the one of the car.' He points to the photo in front of Lallie. A white station wagon with a black roof-rack is parked on the street. There is enough light from the camera flash and the repaired street light for the rear number plate to stand out clearly.

'It can't be ...' she says again.

'What?' Tan asks.

Lallie carries the photo over to the window and

examines it in the bright light. Then she says, 'If I hadn't seen this with my own eyes, I would never have believed it. My son. My own flesh and blood. How *could* he?'

It's Hellz's turn to be stunned.

'Y' mean . . . it's y' son's car?'

'Yes. Unless he's sold it in the last two days. But why . . .?'

'Ask him,' Hellz says.

Lallie hesitates, then she says, 'Yes. Yes, of course,' and goes to the phone.

'I hope I didn't get you out of bed, dear.'

'No, Mother.'

'I was wondering if you had sold your car. The white one, with the black roof-rack.'

'Of course not. Why would I?'

'I really don't know. But I think you had better get yourself around here – immediately.'

'Are you all right, Mother? You haven't had trouble with that prowler again? I *wish* you'd listen to me and move out of that house. It's too dangerous, living there alone.'

'Nonsense! I am perfectly capable. Are you coming, or not?'

'It's not really convenient at the moment.'

'It will be much less convenient if I have to send the police around to pick you up, believe me!'

'The police! Now you really are getting confused, Mother. In the retirement village you would have proper care. Proper security, and people around you. To look after you, you know . . .'

Lallie holds the phone away from her ear for a few moments, then hangs up.

While they wait, Lallie makes tea. 'I know you boys would prefer lemonade.' They both nod their heads. 'I've made a fresh batch. It's in the fridge.' Tan is closest and opens the heavy, old door. 'And you know where the glasses are, Hellz.'

They sit in silence. Lallie's thoughts are obviously miles away. But as the hot, refreshing tea goes down her wrinkled throat she begins to talk.

'He wants me out of the house, you know. Has done for ages. Wants to sell it to that sleazy Elliott Adams creature. Keeps going on about it being too big for me to look after, now. And about how much it's worth.' Her voice wavers, but steadies again. 'Well, no amount of money will entice me to leave my garden. You can't even grow weeds in those poky little units. And what about Winston? You can imagine him having to wipe his feet and blow his nose, can't you?' She pauses thoughtfully. 'Anyway, rough or not, I *like* this neighbourhood. I don't want to die of boredom in a retirement village!' She drains the last of the tea from her cup. 'I suppose he thought if he destroyed my precious garden, I would be so disheartened I'd give in and go.'

'No. You mustn't!' Hellz is horrified at the thought of Lallie giving up her freedom.

She grins. 'Oh, I won't, don't worry. I can always replant the garden.'

Herman arrives in his white station wagon with the distinctive roof-rack. Winston wags his tail and goes to the door with Lallie.

'This is my son, Herman,' Lallie introduces him to Hellz and Tan. Then she turns to Herman and says, 'Meet my new friends. Hellz ...' Herman extends his hand. Hellz shakes it. 'And Tan.' The ritual is repeated. 'The boys have been helping me with a bit of detective work.' She indicates a chair and Herman sits down. Lallie carefully places the photograph of the car in front of him. 'Do you recognise this?'

'Of course I do, Mother. And so do you.'

'Then what was it doing, parked outside *this*

house just after midnight while the most recent attack on my property was in progress?'

'So, that prowler *has* been around again!' Herman gets to his feet. 'Mother, I really must insist . . .'

'Don't change the subject,' Lallie narrows her eyes. 'Were you, or were you not outside my bedroom window at one minute past midnight last night?'

'Mother!' Herman is shocked. 'How could you even *think* such a thing?'

'What else am I to think? Hellz took these photographs *during* the attack! A man of about your build can just be seen running off in this one.' She points it out.

The look on Herman's face changes from outrage to embarrassment.

'Well?' Lallie is impatient.

Herman gives a barely audible gulp and says with quiet amazement, 'I loaned my car to Elliott Adams last night.'

'Elliott Adams!' Lallie crows. 'We *knew* that man could not be trusted. Didn't we, Winston? So *he* is the one who thinks he can frighten me out of my wits *and* my house.'

'I'm really sorry, Mother ...' Herman sags in the chair.

'Never mind, my dear. Just leave it to me, now. *I'll* deal with him.' Lallie thumps her open palm hard on the table. 'And promise me we won't have any more of this moving-out nonsense. This is a *very* safe neighbourhood. I have good friends here.' She turns to Hellz and Tan with a broad smile. 'Besides, we can't have the younger generation growing up without homemade cake, can we?' Hellz gives Lallie a thumbs-up sign and helps himself to another piece, then pushes the plate towards Tan.

There is a knock at the open door.

'Hi. I just thought I'd call and see how the ...' Hellz's mum stops when she sees Herman.

'Come on in, Anna,' Lallie beckons her and she enters the room. Introductions are made and Lallie pours more tea.

'Bring that other chair from under the window, will you Hellz?'

Hellz crosses the room. It's a clear summer's day and the crystal has draped its rainbow across the chair like a discarded scarf. Hellz looks up at the sparkling teardrop. *They're magic, those crystals.*

Eddie's words come back to him. Can it really see into the future? he wonders. And does it see Eddie as part of *his* future? Suddenly the crystal twists in a fresh gust of wind and flashes him a wink of brightness. With fresh air filling his lungs, he picks up the chair and returns to the laughing group at the table, carrying a fragment of the rainbow with him.

ABOUT THE AUTHOR

Elaine Forrestal lives in Perth, Western Australia in a house very like Lallie's and the younger of her two daughters has a dog very like Winston. Her other daughter has two non-skateboarding children. Elaine shares her house with a dog, a cat and her husband, Peter, who is also a writer.

Although she was born in Perth, Elaine has lived in many different places and travelled throughout the world. Apart from Australia she has spent most time in France, Northern Ireland, England and Canada. As a writer and a teacher, she is able to keep in close contact with a wide range of children, and many of her story ideas spring from school experiences. She has had magazine articles and short stories published and has written for children's television. Her novel *The Watching Lake* was shortlisted for the Western Australian Premier's Book Awards, whilst *Someone Like Me* was the winner of the 1998 Children's Book Council of Australia Book of the Year Award for Younger Readers.